The Seven Wonders of Scotland ! WHAT

THE SEVEN WONDERS OF SCOTLAND

ANDREW CRUMEY, MICHAEL GARDINER,
GAVIN INGLIS, BILLY LETFORD, MAGGIE MELLON,
CAROLINE VON SCHMALENSEE
AND KIRSTI WISHART

INTRODUCED BY
GERRY HASSAN

People Making
Waves
Scottish Wave of Change

First published in Great Britain in 2012 by

Birlinn Limited
West Newington House
10 Newington Road
Edinburgh
EH9 1QS

www.birlinn.co.uk

ISBN 978 1 78027 100 2

British Library Cataloguing-in-Publication Data
A catalogue record for this book is available from the British Library.

LOTTERY FUNDED   **LOTTERY FUNDED**

The Scottish Wave of Change is supported by People Making Waves, which is part of the Scottish Project. The Scottish Project has been funded by Legacy Trust UK, creating a lasting impact
from the London 2012 Olympic and Paralympic Games by funding ideas and local talent to inspire creativity across the UK and by the National Lottery through Creative Scotland.

Designed and typeset by Hewer Text Ltd, Edinburgh
Printed and bound by MPG Books Limited, Bodmin

Contents

Scotland's Stories: A Nation of Imaginations

Gerry Hassan

A nation is a soul, a spiritual principle . . . a large scale solidarity, constituted by the feelings of the sacrifices that one has made in the past and of those that one is prepared to make in the future . . . it is summarised however, in the present by a tangible fact, namely, contest, the clearly expressed desire to continue a common life. A nation's existence is, if you will pardon the metaphor, a daily plebiscite.

Ernest Renan, 'What is a Nation?' (1882)

Scotland is a land, country and place filled with stories: memories, myths, folklore and tales, both oral and written.

This book is about the stories of Scotland, exploring different futures of the mind and imagination, and takes us on a journey into familiar and unfamiliar territories which provoke and stimulate. In so doing it reveals something about ourselves, about the Scotland we inhabit in the here and now, and about the possibilities of the future.

This future is shaped by the Scotland of economic change and doubt, social and inter-generational anxieties and cultural transformation. It is the land of the long road to the independence referendum, of Rangers FC passing into liquidation and out of the Scotland Premier League, and of Rupert Murdoch's reach and influence over the Scottish and British political classes, and the politics of the court and courtiers of the last thirty years beginning to unravel. It is about a place where so many assumptions, institutions and beliefs are either crumbling or being called into question.

The Personal and the Collective

Scotland has had many stories about itself – as an imagined space, a different space from the rest of the UK, as an historical nation, and as a mythical, magical place. There is the Scotland of invention, ingenuity and creativity; the Scotland of the mind, the Enlightenment, thinking, inquisitiveness and curiosity; and the Scotland of a political community.

This introduction looks at the themes of this book, puts them into the context of contemporary Scotland and the current debate on our future. One of the book's assumptions (and of this introduction) is the connection between our personal and collective stories. It is important to give voice to our own individual stories, to own them, and acknowledge the importance of lived life and experience.

I was born in Dundee, conscious from an early age that I lived somewhere different from 'the Central Belt' and the seeming metropolis of Glasgow and Edinburgh. Realising that we had to endure Grampian TV rather than STV was my first understanding of this basic geographical fact.

My parents brought me up in the 1970s on a prosperous council estate on the outskirts of Dundee, of which there were many in Scotland. They believed in Britain as a country which was about advancing fairness, wider opportunities and a sense of hope for them, their son, and people like us. Related to this they had a sense of optimism about the future: of the world slowly becoming a better place, made by the collective effort of working people across the world.

Connected to both of these beliefs they had an innate confidence that people like them had the capabilities to bring change through action in trade unions, community activism and wider politics. My father was active in the first and last, working in NCR where he was a shop steward, and a member of the Communist Party, not an unusual phenomenon in Dundee in the 1970s; while my mother was active in running the local community centre and the newspaper, *Ardler News*.

This worldview informed my parents and most of my friends' parents; it was a world of safety, solidarity and being positive; the bad old days of grim poverty and unemployment seen in the 1930s were behind us; the future would be tidy, rational and shaped by enlightened authority. It was more often assumed and unstated most of the time despite the above; it was taken as a given, something that was close to the natural order of things, and that of course, turned out to be a complete misreading of where we were and where we were going.

In my childhood my parents inculcated in me a sense of curiosity, ideas and confidence, of asking questions, challenging quietly, and believing in change. The progress of individual empowerment and collective advance went in tandem for them, but even through the eyes of a child, strains were beginning to show. There were the miners' strikes of 1972 and 1974, the rising divisiveness and bitter politics of the decade, and the

1975 European referendum and 1979 Scots (and Welsh) devolution votes, and the emergence of Mrs Thatcher.

My parents changed their views as the world transformed: my dad moved from a softly spoken Stalinism to Scottish nationalism, and my mum retreated from community politics. I don't think it is an overstatement to say that the three pillars of that 1970s Dundee world seem now like archaeological remains from a lost, long distant age. The demise of those stories has proven difficult and painful for many, but it has also opened up spaces, possibilities and imaginations for a very different kind of Scotland, Britain and world.

What are Modern Scotland's Stories?

What then are Scotland's defining stories at this crucial point in our history? Many of our traditional accounts are suffering from exhaustion, discredited or hollowed out, from the collectivist dreams of salvation from socialism to the belief in religious redemption, both with their sense of either being damned or saved. There are arguably three pivotal accounts present at this time: the Scotland of the egalitarian impulse, the Scotland of the democratic intellect and the nation and culture of popular sovereignty.

This is not the reality of contemporary Scotland. These accounts are defining myths or mobilising myths if you like, which shape who we think we are, define us and our place in the world. They influence our normative values, where we think we came from and are heading, our attitudes, decisions and behaviours. James Mitchell defined myth as 'an idea or set of ideas whose importance lies in being believed or accepted by a significant body of people sufficient to affect behaviour or attitudes whether grounded in fact or fiction'. David McCrone argued that 'the Scottish myth' of egalitarianism is 'not dependent on facts', because it represents a set of social self-evident values, a social ethos, a celebration of sacred beliefs about what it is to be 'Scottish' which provides 'an ideological device for marking off the Scots from the English'.

This book poses seven Scotlands of the future, taking inspiration from Christopher Booker's 'The Seven Basic Plots' which proposes that there are only a certain number of archetypical stories in the world. Booker identified seven, but underneath this he found what he claimed was the one unifying theme, the human search for the light, the threat and power of the darkness and our search for resolution; this takes, us he observed, to the modern-day fixation with the Nazis and the appeal of *Star Wars*.

What do our seven Scotlands tell us about this place, its people and future?

They explore a Scotland which addresses some of its most deep-seated historic problems such as sectarianism, public health, education and poverty.

A future where the past is reimagined, recreated and constantly changing, but which does not prescriptively control or define us. Instead, we live in a culture which thinks about past, present and future, recognising that in any mature reflection all three are interconnected.

Where Scotland becomes a positive international example, using some of the challenges we face as a motivation for change which not only fundamentally transforms lives of people here but contributes to significant changes in knowledge, insight and wisdom much more widely.

A Scotland where the unsustainable nature of the Anglo-American model of capitalism and society, and all the consequences which go with it: inequality, hyper-individualism, the belief in the autonomous self, is seen as flawed, limited and dangerous. This goes beyond negativity and critique to a more complex understanding of human behaviour which is reflected in how society is organised.

A future which has posed and offered answers to some of the deep existential questions about ourselves and the meaning and purpose we want Scotland to nurture, champion and embody. This is a land where the importance of values is centre stage, but no longer is Scottish society drawn to ill-defined abstracts which are never defined but used as distant utopias to aid people being disaffected; instead, our collective values shape the practical principles of society.

A wider set of communal societal stories emerge which address the issues of mission and purpose that come from a powerful sense of 'we' and 'us'; where we are more than a disparate group of individuals or groups but bound together by a sense of mutual obligation and understanding. And that in twenty-first century Scotland, new mobilising myths and perspectives emerge which resonate with our past and connect to a future.

And, finally, a place where the cathedrals of the future chime to the gospel sounds of a variety of Scottish songs that we sing in our own voice, telling our own stories without it being a prescriptive or an official Scotland; a land which recognises the meaning beyond meaning.

The stories represent part of a bigger, more ambitious project – A Scottish Wave of Change – which sat as part of the Cultural Olympiad. A Scottish Wave of Change was a mass imagination project, looking at how we imagine, create and democratise the future, drawing from some of the insights in two previous futures initiatives – Scotland 2020 and Glasgow 2020.

A Scottish Wave of Change developed a host of futures projects across Scotland, bringing together nearly sixty events involving several thousand people; it had three long-term local initiatives in Dundee, Govan and Lochgilphead. These were chosen to develop deep genuine conversations and explorations based on long-term relationships of trust. The three areas reflect very different communities in every way: one a city, one a significant-sized community in Scotland's biggest city, and another a small rural town. Together, they drew on the notion of 'the three Scotlands' – of bringing together and making connections across different communities, geographically, generationally and socio-economically. Each undertook a range of local events, undertaking discussions, initiatives and public engagement from World Café reflections to a learning journey by bus into the future, to creating the local media headlines of tomorrow. This involves making films, plays, music and much more; we brought together 'the three Scotland' strands at several points to aid people in comparing, contrasting and collaborating.

Many other activities took place: a music album of young people's stories of growing up in Scotland; leading playwrights coming together to reflect, write and put on a play about Scotland's future; and a group of young people learning how to work together and sail a boat, building up to sailing around the coast of Scotland, collecting stories and making a film, *Sharing Stories*, with filmmaker Sitar Rose.

This book and the insights of A Scottish Wave of Change have created change and developed resources, ideas and connections which will outlive the time span of this project. Let me turn now to some of the general insights which have emerged.

Three Defining Scottish Stories

What drives and motivates much of Scotland's debate, from its politics, to the constitutional debate, our distinct and different public realm, and culture, identities and understanding of history, is a desire to develop and create distinct collective stories in which we see ourselves.

To understand and connect between past, present and future, I suggest we return to the three mobilising, defining myths mentioned earlier: the egalitarian impulse, the democratic impulse and popular sovereignty.

Over recent times Scots have comforted themselves with the belief that we are not like England and that we have comprehensively rejected the excesses of Anglo-American capitalism. The implication is that we are more virtuous, moral and filled with a mission of compassion, honour and duty: a sort of 'love thy neighbour' attitude as evidenced in William McIlvanney's 1980s pronouncements about Thatcherism and the Scots sense of community.

Scotland is shaped by an egalitarian impulse, Jock Tamson's bairns and all that, yet Scotland is one of the most unequal places in the developed world. We are only marginally less unequal than England, itself distorted by the existence of London, the most unequal city in the world. The UK is the fourth most unequal country in the developed world, only surpassed by the USA, Portugal and Singapore.

Then there is the evoking of the democratic intellect, of pride in Scotland's curiosity of the mind, its inquisitiveness in relation to ideas, and our generalist educational traditions which many believe are more open and meritocratic than England. This is the world of the all-pervasive myth. The Scottish education system with its lad o'pairts was never this hallowed world of liberation, was never particularly child-orientated or friendly, and has in recent decades, become a virtually closed system, complacent, inward-looking and shaped by organised interests.

Finally, there is the most powerful account of Scotland in recent times: that of the sovereignty of the people and of popular sovereignty. This argument believes that Scotland as a distinct political and historical space – from the Declaration of Arbroath of 1320 to MacCormick v. Lord Advocate in 1953 and 'A Claim of Right' in 1988 – is a nation where instead of parliamentary sovereignty the tradition and practice is of popular sovereignty. It draws on the notion of the different titles of the monarch north and south of the border: in England the monarch was always the King or Queen of England, whereas in Scotland they were King or Queen of Scots; in the former their authority comes from the tradition of absolutism, whereas in the latter, it supposedly derives from the people.

Scotland is, of course, not in any legal or literal political way a place of popular sovereignty. If it were our society, democracy and culture would look very different. The experience of Thatcher, the democratic deficit and the poll tax would have all been substantially mitigated and resisted. The talking shop that was the Scottish Constitutional Convention of the 1980s would have been more than an alternative elite Scotland. More crucially, our democratic practices would be more varied and concerned with the 'forgotten Scotland' and missing voices who are excluded from democratic politics. There would be in a culture shaped by popular sovereignty a whole raft of processes and practices by which the peoples' will and voices were expressed: referenda, deliberative and participative forums, and a diffusing and dispersing of power beyond the political realm and classes; that is not the Scotland of today.

If Scotland wants to be true to how many people see it and imagine it, then it needs to change dramatically from the current situation and practices; and the best way of doing that, of building wide enough support for change is to go with the grain of some of our existing traditions. That is, after all, what the forces of power and privilege have done these last thirty years: from New Labour and the Cameron Conservatives to the market fundamentalists across the globe.

A Scotland that was shaped and acted upon these three myths would be a place which sat in the proud tradition of the inventors and imagineers, agitators, provocateurs and radicals of our past. A more egalitarian society would start to care and act upon the seismic inequalities, economic, social and cultural, which disfigure our nation. How can we be an egalitarian society when so many people are excluded from gaining work, opportunities or genuine choice, where our health inequalities are the worst in Western Europe, and our democracy is shrunken and atrophied with so many Scots silenced and ignored?

A society of the democratic intellect would be one which began to rethink learning and education, and embrace the insights and implications of psychology. We would begin to move from uncritically accepting the power of rationality, systems and a narrow notion of knowledge and intelligence, and begin to understand that the world is rather more messy, complex and unpredictable: that intelligence comes in many different forms, and that we have to understand the power of the emotional, the subjective and the subconscious.

Finally, in popular sovereignty we would begin to challenge the over-prescriptive, tightly controlled bandwidth of what it is possible to imagine politically and as the popular will. Instead, we would endlessly experiment with different formats, learn how to use humour, play and irreverence, and encourage spaces and resources which sit outside the system. We would do something about the missing Scotland which in places has been excluded for the last thirty years and, as importantly, we would begin to establish some basic rules about how and who should conduct a modern democracy: how we can appropriately agree and disagree constructively, challenge disrespect, exclusion and the generational, gender and socio-economic gridlock which disfigures our public life.

The Languages of the Future Scotland

This brings us back to some of the central findings from A Scottish Wave of Change and something which emerged continually in some of the Dundee, Govan and Lochgilphead conversations. This is the language of social change; the underlying philosophy that is relevant and apposite to the challenges we face.

Time and again in discussions people reflected upon the importance or uniqueness of a revelation and its potential insights; time and again they then ruminated that the existing language and assumptions of the world were completely inadequate to allow them to fully capture and explain it. In particular, many people felt there was a crucial missing dimension between talking about a unique experience or insight in the local or particular, and explaining it and giving it form with regard to the national or general.

This tells us something about the current age we live in; the exhaustion of the old Enlightenment stories, the hollowing out and collapse of modernity and its associated clarion calls, progress and rationality. An important caveat is that our narrow, technocratic, managerialist political classes still shape their debates to these reference points and measurements, but beyond them and their immediate circles, few people believe in their hearts that this is the way to understand society.

Much of the languages that we still use in everyday political life to describe much of our political world is the language of yesteryear. They have been shorn of most of their meaning and yet we retain them as a tribute to a past age of certainty and for want of anything better. Perhaps even more serious and damaging is the language and words of the new elite and nomenclature: modernisation, competition, change, the status quo is not an option, world class, drilling down, and other innocent sounding descriptions which disguise their intention. This has become the age of a new concentration of power, privilege and wealth, and a host of apologists and bloviators.

We have to begin to give shape to a new language and landscape in twenty-first century Scotland and globally: one which is focused on social change, on organic, evolving, messy forces and transformation, not the language of the system, institutions or elites. This will have to address the challenge of power, who has it and who doesn't, and of voice, who has it and who doesn't. And in a pluralist mature society we have to recognise the possibilities and limits of politics, and address cultural, philosophical and psychological dimensions.

That language would be centred in Scotland around the ideals of self-determination, for individuals, communities and society. In drawing from some of our most powerful traditions and ideas, it would recognise that we are a deeply conservative, cautious society. In rejecting the idea that politics is everything it would also challenge the narrow notion of change as being just about politicians and political institutions. This would mean that debate stopped focusing nearly exclusively on the Scottish Parliament (and the choice seemingly ranging from it gaining full powers under independence to greater powers under other plans). Behind most of the language of 'independence' and 'devolution' is an assumption of political change in terms of the political elites; in particular, the latter word has become one used by an elite talking to itself about securing more power and status for itself; we should instead think of a Scotland beyond devolution.

Scotland has over recent decades been on a journey of self-government – one which is about us as a nation, which has focused too narrowly on politics, politicians and institutions, while pretending otherwise in rhetoric, referencing how radical we are and invoking myths such as popular sovereignty.

A culture and vision of self-determination would involve cultural change and a shift in our collective psychology. Self-determination is about what we imagine our society should be like, our collective future, and how we nurture individuals and communities. Importantly, self-determination draws from respected authoritative set of ideas from around the world, which addresses what individuals need to prosper, thrive and be happy and secure in society, namely, autonomy, competence and relatedness. These three basic building blocks are the key ingredients in modern life in complex societies; and we can reflect that across too much of contemporary Scotland, these factors are missing from too many people's lives. We have, despite our rhetoric, a self-determination deficit.

A Scotland with an active confident self-determination movement would be able to have a much more relevant and substantial debate about the possibilities of self-government. What is stopping us from making this shift is the gridlock in part of our politics, and the institutional inertia and stasis in large swathes of our society. That is the challenge of not only the next few years as we head to the independence referendum of 2014, but for Scotland in the first part of the twenty-first century.

The Long Revolutions

Scotland's journey to its current place has been a long one – one where Scots took a series of decisions long before the arrival of the SNP in government from 2007 onward. This has been an evolving environment from the period of late Victorian Britain when a set of decisions were undertaken which slowly began to put in place a distinct Scottish administrative space in the form of the establishment of the Secretary of State for Scotland and then the government department, the Scottish

Office. These marked out that Scotland was different, a territorial space which could take semi-autonomous decisions, lobby in government and sometimes in public.

This administrative space then increasingly became a politically contested terrain, with arguments and disagreements over government policy and decisions. This increased pressure for the Scottish dimension of politics and government to be democratically accountable, leading to the campaign for a Scottish Parliament, and the 1979 and 1997 devolution referendums. These saw the eventual establishment of the Scottish Parliament in 1999 which gave the SNP a platform, made it the main opposition to Labour, and provided the context to make the case for independence and greater self-government more plausible.

Therefore, it is important to understand this context: the long story and the fact that Scots made a number of key decisions years ago which have shaped and led inexorably to where we are now. It is often thus with totemic decisions and subjects: namely that the crucial, defining decisions were taken much earlier than anyone imagined. Examples of this include America's involvement in the Vietnam War which began under Eisenhower in the 1950s and Britain's historically troubled relationship with the European Union which has from the 1970s made a future in/out referendum more than likely. Similarly from the end of the nineteenth century, the contours of Scottish politics, society and government have been shaped by the dynamics and pressures for self-government and within that independence; the current state of Scotland has much deeper roots than the popularity and positioning of any one party or politician.

Modern Scotland is not a land of continuous serious deliberation, political discussion and historical reflection. It is also shaped by a host of other factors: the ephemera of everyday life, popular culture and the multiple ways in which people can define themselves. Neal Gabler in his book *Life: The Movie* makes the argument that, over the course of the last century, the rise of the entertainment industry has dramatically changed many aspects of our lives, from politics to media, to how we consume and think about consuming, and personal identities. People, argued Gabler, increasingly see themselves as actors in a movie which stars themselves, and think of their lives –their relationships, choices and dilemmas – in cinematic terms. This process, he believes, has fundamentally altered the nature of society and politics in ways which are far-reaching; politics, for example, has become shaped by the notion of 'the narrative', to control it and maintain its consistency and core message. Media reporting has increasingly followed the same direction, emphasising plots, individual stories and real-life experiences.

Scotland: The Movie might have a dramatic appeal, title and potential, but this world is a double-edged sword. Yes, it offers scope for framing, reaching new audiences and having an emotional reach, but there is also the pitfall of potential simplification, dumbing down, and a blurring of fact and fiction. Scotland has already invoked a huge range of myths and folklore from Brigadoon to *Braveheart*, and modern media has the prospect of locating much of the debate in this territory.

The respected authority on screenwriting Robert McKee's magnum opus, *Story*, examines what makes and draws us into a story, principally, the importance of character. He writes that it is 'revealed in the choices a human being makes under pressure

– the greater the pressure, the deeper the revelation, the truer the choice to the character's essential nature'. Pivotal to this is the issue of risk according to McKee: 'Here's a simple test to apply to any story. Ask: what is the risk? What does the protagonist stand to lose if he does not get what he wants? More specifically, what's the worst thing that will happen to the protagonist if he does not achieve his desire? If this question cannot be answered in a compelling way, the story is misconceived at its core.'

The idea of story at the level of a nation and society just like in other settings cannot be compelling without people identifying with and embracing risk, change and uncertainty, and in so doing defining their character. It involves understanding whose voices are loudest, who is speaking and missing from debates, and who has been silenced or marginalised; why some stories emerge and become defining, and why others are side-lined and ignored.

Post-war Scotland and the Power of Infinite Scotlands

The recent history of Scotland has seen several distinct phases in relation to collective stories. There was the post-war era of hope, raised ambitions, opportunity and a belief in fairness and progress: the age of planned freedom and the state as an enabler and a maker of possibilities in a society of order, certainty and solidarity. This was then superseded by a more unpredictable world from the 1980s onward, shaped by individual choice, go-getting entrepreneurs and a decline in deference and belief in authority, which was hugely contentious in Scotland, and from which many people gained and more lost out.

Much of the prevailing mood of discussion in Scotland and the UK dwells on a sense of how we have lost something precious, as if previous eras were ones of either great innocence or somehow more nobler. Those feelings existed before the recent challenges of the crash, global crisis and age of austerity. They show us that there has been a significant disconnect between how people live and experience their own personal lives, shaped by opportunity and hope, and the absence of convincing collective stories.

This is the terrain of Scotland's future stories. Recognising the richness, engagement and hope which fill many personal lives, while addressing the need for collective stories, agency and action. These new stories will be located in the longer story of Scotland – from Victorian times to today, and they will also have to relate to the story of post-war Scotland, of the shift from the immediate post-1945 era feeling of 'We Have a Dream' to the 1980s belief that 'We are all doomed', two very powerful Scottish archetypes, of abstract utopias and depowerment.

Scotland's future is about greater self-government but it has to be about more than that to involve, engage and inspire. This is about a vision of a society, culture and economy shaped by the principles of self-determination, in which we learn how to express our individual and collective desires and hopes in a manner which acknowledges the fragilities of the planet and the impermanence of the human race.

Telling these stories necessitates that we start to leave the closed conversations, comforting stories and vested interest positions of much of modern Scotland; that we take the risk of challenging the narrow bandwidth and self-interest of institutional Scotland; that we recognise the limited nature of much of what passes for 'civic Scotland', but in reality is a set of gatekeepers, aiding the continuation of undemocracy and unspace, practices and places where it is difficult to impossible to nurture honest, reflective discussion and ideas.

The old stories which defined us and contributed so much to making us are threadbare and exhausted, and in the eyes of most, discredited or simply irrelevant. We have to nurture, nourish and aid into being new stories which succeed in a very delicate balancing act: embracing complexity, but allowing for some simplicity, daring to be daring, allowing ourselves to be indignant at the state of much of our society, but not falling into hectoring and lecturing; and allowing for joy and lightness in a world where so much is unjust and needs to be challenged, but where much of life is worth celebrating and affirming; and allowing for these nuances.

This will require that Scotland's storytellers engage with the future of society, from writers, musicians, imagineers and historians to other radical and disruptive forces. It will need iconoclastic voices to be encouraged to offer challenging accounts to 'the official future' and prevailing myths; interventions of the originality and verve of Momus's unique *The Book of Scotlands* where he developed a whole panoply of parallel Scotlands of the imagination; or in the work of Andy Wightman who has forensically mapped the patterns and inequities of land ownership and pointed out the strange Scottish lack of curiosity about power. Then there is filmmaker Anthony Baxter's award-winning documentary *You've Been Trumped*, chronicling the excesses and abuses of Donald Trump building his Scottish golf course on the Menie Estate. And this year has seen 'the Scottish spring' of football fans standing up against the institutional interests and for a fundamentally different vision of the national game.

This involves understanding the past Scottish futures, their hopes and how they ultimately failed. Most important are the two most recent, the post-1945 era and that of the 1980s onward. The first involved an explicit 'eye to the future' and belief that the Scotland of tomorrow would be a more enlightened, fairer and better place, and that a new kind of world and society was possible. A vision of this, *The Future of Scotland*, written in 1939 stated:

> For that we require vision. Short-sighted hand-to-mouth legislation is useless. Procrastination is equally dangerous and indefensible. The organisation essential to put things through, it should be remembered, will not spring into being of itself and even if it did, it would be of no avail without a reawakened popular consciousness.

These words are equally true in the Scotland of the twenty-first century. Our challenges entail that we think and act boldly, and are radical about how we think and create the future. Fundamental to how we imagine, dream and create a different Scotland will be our stories and storytellers and what has been called 'the community of communicators'. The stories in this book offer a tantalising stimulating journey, a rich mosaic which reflects and conveys this challenge. There is the hidden underground Scotland of Andrew Crumey, where the archaeological remains of the past has an almost mythical power. Then we have a modern-day independent Scotland which became so a century ago, according to William Letford, where Loch Lomond is the world's first semi-submerged city.

In Caroline van Schmalensee's contribution a new community emerges in a prototype to reduce global warning and begins an experiment in living with wider repercussions; Kirsti Wishart draws from the Scottish International Exhibitions of Victoriana to the People's Palace and even Las Vegas to examine pleasure; and Maggie Mellon envisages Glasgow as a post-industrial urban garden town. Gavin Inglis paints a country which has confronted one of its most difficult and shameful aspects – religious bigotry; and Michael Gardiner enters a dystopian Anglo-America which is increasingly seen as such, and outside of which Scotland explicitly and proudly stands.

Returning to my own experience of growing up in Dundee and that of my parents, one of the powerful anchors was how they saw their own life and future and its connection with wider possibilities. There was a tension and a balance in this, and as people grew more questioning and affluent many in Scotland felt that we overdid the latter, the sense of the collective, at the expense of the individual.

The post-war era contained for my parents a sense of optimism, but that was only part of the picture. What we now seem to have shifted to in many accounts is a story of the present day filled with loss, despair, pessimism and a longing for a golden age which never was. Just as the immediate post-war years were not all sweetness and consensus, so the present is not all discord and darkness.

This points to the profound disconnect between personal experience and the public life of society and the nation. The way in which most people describe their individual lives and that of their immediate families is informed by a belief that, whatever the current economic and social problems, life can and will eventually get better. However, at the level of the collective, we seem to have a deep failure to articulate these hopes and wishes, and find plausible vessels and accounts in which people believe. This disconnect, and how it is addressed, is crucial if the possible Scotlands of the future are to emerge and take shape.

Language is pivotal. The dominant ideas of the last few decades, across the political spectrum – abstractions such as 'globalisation', 'free market values', 'inequality' and 'poverty' – mean little to most people. Instead, future stories need to connect the individual to the collective, and concern relationships and the values we choose to cherish. Thus, instead of talking in the abstract about economic growth, we would address how people get on in their lives and support themselves and their families. The same would be true of how we conceive of poverty, inequality and other social issues.

This may seem a small step to some and an obtuse point to others but I would suggest that the prevalence of system talk, thinking and jargon does not allow for the articulation of deeper values and ideas, and the search for new understandings and philosophies. Many people intrinsically recognise this mismatch and the resultant hollowing out of public life.

This would be a Scotland of mission and purpose, collective stories and utopian imagination, and going with the grain of our character and culture as the most likely way to aid change. What this leads to is the following question: what has a small cohesive nation at the cusp of a historic debate and decision to lose by being bold, drawing from the best of our traditions, trying to aspire to the noblest in them, and learning from others in a similar situation? We have so much to gain: in short, a future that we make ourselves, can call our own and contribute to the wider world.

The Burrows

Andrew Crumey

Is it monument or burden? From somewhere came the urge to replace bulk solidity with weightless void. Our forebears chose to dig.

The Burrows had their origin in what was considered at the time a combination of impulses: educational, patriotic, artistic, commercial. Nowadays we might think all of them a subset of the philosophical, bracketed within that era's presiding spirit: random curiosity or grandiose boredom. What would they find down there with their excavating machines? What might they add? So many tunnels and passages existed already; mines closed and abandoned, underground railways, nuclear bunkers and silos, entire streets built over and forgotten. A dark, disconnected world of caves, cellars and subways, a labyrinth awaiting the unifying power of thought and the labour that would make it real. A second nation below the surface.

Some saw it primarily as tourist attraction, a well for foreign coin. For others it would be a scientific quest or spiritual journey. At what depth below the Earth's surface do you start to feel the fires of Hell? With the finest equipment available, and with the most supreme effort, might a shaft pierce the planet's soft core? Nationalists asserted Scotland's right to determine its subterranean affairs, opponents pointed out that the size of any country must shrink with increasing depth, the centre is where all borders meet and dissolve, a geo-political singularity. It was rumoured that the Russians had got there already. Why not the sky instead? The area that calls itself Scotland must surely increase with altitude, go far enough and it will embrace numerous stellar systems. But the cash ran out. So down they went.

The initial phase was a linking of existing underground spaces with new passages. The first was meant to run from Mary King's Close to St Ninian's Cave but navigational problems emerged almost as soon as the contractors began tunnelling: they hadn't realised their sat nav wouldn't work underground. They had to fall back on traditional surveying techniques, and old digging methods too, when an industrial dispute brought the giant screw-nosed machine to a shuddering halt. In the end it was local schoolchildren who scooped out the last of the earth between Edinburgh and Whithorn, while householders along the entire route took legal action over subsiding homes and disappearing gardens.

It might all have ended there, were it not for a discovery made during the tunnelling. At a location somewhere beneath Sanquhar post office a temporary restroom needed to be installed and a side passage was created. Engineers noticed something strange about the rock they encountered, geologists took soundings, revealing a large chamber of strangely regular proportions. Earth was moved and the unusual rock revealed as ancient building stone, enclosing an empty hall of unknown purpose, devoid of any artefact save a small corroded metal disc.

'What does it mean?' the head of operations was asked by a television news reporter when news leaked out.

'It means we're not the first.'

There were suggestions that the submerged room was a nineteenth-century folly but there was no way to prove it. Fantasists were quick to invent outlandish explanations: the metal disc, it was said, had been fashioned from a meteorite. But now there was a new impetus to excavate, and donations came from Scots around the world, or at any rate people who considered themselves Scots. Litigant householders found that their collapsed dwellings had suddenly acquired a new cachet and increased market value. Properties were advertised, offering extensive views of the underground they had fallen into, made attractive by easy transport connection to the capital, just as soon as they got the mini-train running inside the tunnel. In the meantime it was foot or mule, a healthy and environmentally attractive option.

There was another Scotland down there, waiting to be dug out, mapped, inhabited. Its discovery and colonisation would entail the linking of every surface entrance: the network was to be as thorough and complete as the road system above ground. In any cellar there would be a door, some further steps and then the cool passageway that could lead wherever the stroller wished to venture; softly illuminated walkways of pleasantly curved cross-section, ceramically tiled, along which electric cars could hum peacefully at moderate speed. It wasn't long before everyone was calling it the Burrows – or Burghs, for here was a subterranean community in its own right, demanding proper dwellings, services, schools and hospitals, political autonomy, even independence.

Much of the work, it transpired, had been done already, by whoever was there before. The metal discs turned up frequently, assumed to be money, jewellery, religious symbols or gaming tokens. Archaeology was rewritten: the old assumption was that the deeper you dug, the further back in time you went. This stratified view could no longer be sustained: history, it was realised, is an infinite superposition, all times being present at every point. Certainly the excavators unearthed layers of distinct eras, but only down to a certain limit, beyond which everything was too jumbled to be worth worrying about. If a new chamber was broken into, no one asked any longer if it was a hundred or a thousand years old, or even if it was one that had been dug the previous year and forgotten about. What mattered was its emptiness, its ability to be entered and imagined.

For many people the Burrows became just another place to shop. The chain stores were quick to move in when the first licences were granted, their rows of premises looking no different from any covered mall, quickly reached by high-speed lifts whose occupants would barely notice whether they were going down or up, transfixed in aluminium compartments by illuminated characters declaring an alphabet of levels, more conducive to throughput and spending than numbers, it was found. After a strenuous afternoon of retail there could be the relaxation of pub, cinema or restaurant, with no one ever noticing the absence of daylight or the air's particular taste.

Potholers insisted on the benefits of the great below-floors: a popular route started just behind the Marks and Spencers eight hundred and fifty feet beneath Comrie. Guidebooks described how the ramble would soon take you away from the brashly lit shopping centre, past a waterworks, to a dimly lit unsurfaced section requiring sensible footwear and waterproof clothing. Here could be seen glittering stalactites and enough smooth slabs to allow for picnicking if all the benches should happen to be occupied (a frequent occurrence at weekends). But go further, the guides insisted, beyond the realm of daytrippers, carrying a torch and spare batteries, and wearing a hard hat in case of bumps. A natural fissure in the rocks, easily managed by all except the most morbidly rotund, led into a cavern so large that no one had ever been able to shine a beam all the way to the other end, or so it was said. Here the air was clear, cool and pure: breathe deeply and you would feel better in an instant. The place was believed to have been a thriving village once, and Robert the Bruce passed through on the way somewhere. Or maybe it was Mary, Queen of Scots. At any rate, that's what it said on the notice someone put up there.

Thanks to its alleged health-giving properties, Burrows water became a bestselling brand above ground. Some international medical authorities insisted that being starved of sunlight would cause long-term health problems but the Scots had been managing like that for centuries and it hadn't done them any harm. Even so, a variety of strange, unique conditions began to appear, attributable to troglodytic life. The Burrovians' skin was pale, their eyes smaller though with larger pupils. Bone density was found to be greater in comparison with surface people. Perhaps a new race was evolving, or an old one had been reborn. The issue was delicate: should one speak of race at all? A sinister underground movement was found to be emerging, whose members claimed to be whiter than white. Comparisons with sheets of paper and Polo mints showed they actually had a point. Given sufficiently many generations, it was claimed, the Burrow-folk would eventually become translucent, with skin like rice paper and internal organs made visible by anything stronger than fluorescent strip lighting. Continue the evolutionary progression and the result would be total transparency, the disappearance of eyes, a complete adaptation to underground existence.

There were accidents in the Burrows. The very first casualty was Mr Ian Seggie, inspector of operations on a northern stretch of the early phase of tunnelling, who was supervising a subsea link between the Grain Earth-House at Kirkwall and Shebster Cairn near Thurso. There had been much debate about this particular route which posed extreme technical problems, needing to be carved through difficult rock beneath many fathoms of tempestuous ocean. Quite a few people couldn't see any point in it at all, and were invited to attend free public education classes that helped them understand the error of their ways. Mr Seggie, moreover, is reported to have been a 'difficult' type, which would partly explain why progress was so slow, even once his team found a way to stop the tunnel continually flooding with seawater. An official enquiry held after the incident that claimed Seggie's life found that over a period of weeks he had gradually lost all confidence in his workforce, their machinery and the navigational methods they used. He had, in short, decided that the best way to tunnel from Orkney to Caithness was to drive the excavator himself and use his own judgement about which way to steer. His widow Edith summed him up as being a person who would never ask directions from anyone, no matter how lost he became, which the enquiry panel considered to be no explanation at all since it applied to any man. The report instead highlighted the misfortune of a wrongly aligned burrowing screw that meant the vehicle would rise by one centimetre for every three metres travelled horizontally. This, they decided, was the reason why Mr Seggie, on his lone progress beneath the sea floor, found himself worming out of the dark safety of old red sandstone and into the perils of the Pentland Firth. Death, however, was by no means instantaneous: he was found to be wearing a diving suit, a precaution Edith thought entirely characteristic of her late husband who liked to be prepared for any possibility, no matter how remote. One of his foibles, it emerged at the enquiry, was a lightning conductor built into his folding umbrella, with a wire trailing down to earth, just in case. How ironic, then, that he did not think to take it with him underground. When Seggie bored up into the ocean it was not the water that killed him, but the 33,000-volt electricity cable his machine cut through as it roamed along the seabed in search of a good way of getting back down again. Orcadians noticed a brief, inexplicable dimming of their lights, and a trawler skipper who happened to be in the area reported an unusual boiling effect on the sea surface. Such was Seggie's brief mark on history.

There were to be many more fatalities in the Burrows, though when one looks at the statistics, being underground is actually slightly safer than life on the surface. There are, for example, far fewer cases of pneumonia down there. Some attribute this to the lack of rain, though it's more likely due to the lack of pneumonia. One disturbing figure, though, is the suicide rate. The unfortunate trend began soon after the opening of the Pre-Cambrian Experience, a theme park designed to transport visitors into the geological past, long before the emergence of human life. It was not the thought of primordial non-existence that troubled visitors, rather it was the temptation of a dark shaft exposed by construction work, of incalculable depth and unknown origin. Infra-red security cameras revealed that people were showing up at the Pre-Cambrian Experience with the specific intention of throwing themselves down what became known locally as 'the plughole'.

The solution was obvious: fence it off and cover it up. But doing the obvious has never been the way of the Burrows. A team of investigators decided that covering the hole would treat only the symptom, not the problem. To understand the plughole one needed first of all to know how it came to be there in the first place. Was it a natural feature, a volcanic fissure? Had it been created by those forgotten folk with their metal discs? Or accidentally blasted out while cave-scaping the area to accommodate the rollercoaster in the Pre-Cambrian Experience?

Experienced human resources manager Linda Waddell was tasked with going down to have a look. Her brave effort proved unsuccessful: the rope was only a hundred metres long and left Linda dangling in her hard-hat and orange safety-wear with no sign of solid ground beneath, merely a fine mist revealed by the swinging beam of her head-torch. Her supervisor radioed to say they were going to get another length of rope and tie it on, they'd only be about half an hour, but Linda declared she'd had enough, this was never in her job description.

Two weeks later, underground parachutist Clive Knoll stepped in to help. The sport of hole-diving was at this time still in its early days, with only a few drops known to be large enough to accommodate it. The plughole was an obvious challenge for Clive, who edged to the black unfathomable rim wearing a video camera on his helmet and his life's hopes on his back. The whole thing was sponsored by Sleeptight Bedspreads and relayed live on BurrowVision. Clive gave a thumbs-up to the camera, pulled his goggles over his eyes, then a moment later launched himself into the void. The feed from his helmet-cam showed near-total obscurity, with maybe a wee bit of the mist they'd seen before from Linda's attempt. But it was the last that anyone saw of Clive Knoll. How the devil did he expect to get back up again? Sleeptight Bedspreads went into liquidation not long afterwards.

It was suggested that the power of the plughole might merely be conceptual: a mental womb. Celebrity philosopher Angus de Mouchoir made it the subject of a four-part mini-series and accompanying book. A highpoint of the Burrows Festival of Ideas was his appearance at the plughole, where he promised to show that the thing existed only in people's minds. And that was the last anyone heard of him too.

A scientific investigation was commissioned, with backing from International Biscuits who apparently thought the shape of the thing could be utilised in their packaging and marketing, or else maybe wondered if the plughole could serve as a convenient means of disposing of all the waste their underground factories produced along with a cloying buttery smell that many Burrovians found appetising but which was widely suspected to be carcinogenic. The scientists lowered various instruments on ropes and cables and decided that none of the ropes and cables were long enough. Robotic probes fell to oblivion. Some commentators reckoned this was worse than the bloody space race, and look where Scotland had ended up over that nonsense (a space station that fell foul of Friday-night rowdiness, best forgotten).

The only way was to send someone climbing down it. A public competition yielded a shortlist of experienced sub-alpinists, skilled in tackling the steepest and most scenically negative of slopes. The contenders all had fine beards and good musculature, the clear winner by phone-in poll being Annie Thromnick, who impressed everyone in the live final by managing to descend two hundred feet with her hands and feet tied together, using only her teeth to hold onto the rope (it was suggested in some less generous quarters that her success was owed in part to a sympathy vote when people saw the friction burns on her lips – her gran's on-air rendition of Burrovian folk-songs may also have generated some sentimental support).

Annie's de-scaling of the plughole proved however to be a muted media event. Everyone expected her to disappear after thirty seconds like the rest had done, even International Biscuits thought it best to remove their corporate banners temporarily from the mouth of the hole. But Annie was a cut below her predecessors, her heart and spirit belonged to the great depths she loved and was determined to plumb. Quickly chewing her way through the CaveBix she was required to consume as preparation for the ordeal, and watched by a few dozen experts, dignitaries and folk with nothing better to do of an afternoon, she lowered herself

down the vertiginous wall, almost glasslike in its smooth-
ness but with just enough unevenness to give purchase to
the virtuoso descender.

Five minutes passed and half the people went away (there
was a red-carpet event to celebrate the new Library of Comedy,
an archive and celebration of everything that had ever made
anyone laugh, anywhere). Another five minutes of looking at
watches, head-shaking and whistling, and it was generally
agreed that Annie was done for. So the rest went too, though
by this time the red-carpet thing was pretty much done
anyway. It was not until three days later that an exhausted
Annie heroically lifted herself over the lip of the plughole and
was noticed by a wandering Alsatian dog that was being looked
for by Suhindra Wylie, 15, who was caring for it while its
owners were on holiday in the Overland. Suhindra told report-
ers that she thought Annie was a heap of old International
Biscuits packaging because of all the signage around her, until
the heap smiled, revealing a mouth strangely reshaped by friction burns.

During a full debriefing at Burrows Central Infirmary,
Annie revealed the miracle of the plughole. On the first day,
she said, it was pretty much a standard descent, until she
reached a ledge wide enough to rest on. Allowing herself half
a CaveBic and a portion of Deep Spring Water, she accidentally switched off her lamp and was surprised to find that her
surroundings remained illuminated. The rock, she said was
exuding a uniform crepuscular luminescence, a bit like what
you see if you close your eyes and push on your eyeballs. As
she said this, the three scientists at her bedside shut their eyes
and tried it for themselves, pleasantly entertained by what

they saw. The other scientists were away at the Comedy Library and missed the whole thing.

Dr Phoebe Signorelli of the Institute of Geology asked Annie, 'Why did you squeeze your eyeballs when you were down the plughole?'

'I didn't,' said Annie. 'That's what it looked like.'

'You mean someone else squeezed them?'

Professor Vanguard Pym intervened. 'Nobody squeezed anything.'

'We just did . . .'

'Tell us more, Annie,' the Professor instructed.

So Annie described how she waited on the ledge for a considerable time, regaining her strength and allowing her vision to adjust more and more to the strange luminosity around her. Eventually it was bright enough for her to read the health warning on the side of her CaveBix packet. Phoebe Signorelli had meanwhile been squeezing her eyeballs so much that she was advised to go away and sit down. She bumped into the door jamb on the way out and needed some medical attention that rather distracted from Annie's gripping account. The other two decided they'd hear the rest of it next day when they were more in the mood.

It was around this time that Dave Vinsky and his wife Shehalagh returned from their holiday and came to collect their Alsatian dog from Suhindra Wylie. They brought with them souvenirs of the Overland, a pair of deeply offensive suntans, and news that the folk up there were a bigoted and spiteful lot who never said a word to each other on public transport. Not only that, but a person in the queue for the Ben Nevis Aurora Borealis Stagecoach Monorail had the effrontery to say the Burrows didn't even exist!

'You think it's a hoax or something?' Dave Vinsky challenged.

'I'm saying you're not a separate country, you're part of Scotland.'

'But we've got our own laws and education system and football team and everything else.'

'Aye, like language,' Shehalagh chipped in.

'You talk the same language as me,' said the offensive queue-person who was dressed in the internationally recognisable uniform of a lollipop man, must have been his break or something, maybe it was the school holidays.

'What do you call this, then?' said Vinsky, drawing from his wallet a Burrows bank note.

'Piece of paper, still the same currency.'

'Worth more underground though.'

'Worth bugger all here, that's for sure.'

This enjoyable friendly banter went on for the whole time they waited in the queue, and also while the three of them rode the monorail together (there was no aurora that day – too cloudy and the machine had a fault anyway). But afterwards Dave Vinsky was pained by a lingering thought. Lying beside Shehalagh in their mid-price Glasgow hotel bed he asked his snoring wife, 'Do you think he's maybe right? Do you think the Burrows don't exist?'

This was still far from the minds of Professor Vanguard Pym and his assistant Sally who showed up at Annie Thromnick's bed next morning to hear the rest of her story, after they told her about the gig at the Comedy Library.

Annie rested on the ledge for several hours, puzzling over the easily legible health warning on her CaveBix packet that she'd somehow never noticed before. At some moments it became easier to read, then harder, then easier again.

'Were you squeezing your eyeballs?' asked Phoebe Signorelli, who'd arrived late.

Annie explained that the inexplicable phosphorescence was changing colour, passing through shades of lime, mustard, topaz, burgundy. This really confused Phoebe who soon went away again. Annie was a bit freaked too, she lay on the ledge wondering if the nausea she felt was a result of psychedelic illumination or CaveBix. In the end she tried to stand up, but her head immediately throbbed, her heart raced, she lost her balance. 'Everything was spinning and I thought, this is it, Annie, you're going to fall over the side and die.'

'And did you?'

'I threw myself down onto the ledge.'

'That was sensible.'

But the ledge felt different this time, and the colours all around her were creating mental confusion. 'I vomited.'

Professor Vanguard Pym called for the nurse to sort it out, then realised Annie was referring to what happened in the plughole. 'You threw up?'

'No,' said Annie. 'I vomited. But it didn't come up, or spew down.'

Phoebe had only just come back into the room but went straight back out again.

'You see, there was no up or down. It was like gravity had cancelled itself out or something.'

'So where did the vomit go?'

It stayed, she declared, in the air, like a mushy ball of CaveBix.

'That's disgusting,' said Sally.

'Fascinating!' the Professor exclaimed. 'If there was no gravity then that can only mean you had reached the centre of the Earth.'

'Not in a day, though,' said Annie.

'I guess not.'

Dave Vinsky went to work as usual as security consultant at BounceCorp, a leading blue-chip supplier of entrance control personnel, otherwise known as doormen. His task that day was to supervise a red-carpet event at the new Comedy Library, but as he waited for the electric limousine to emerge from Tunnel A52 and deposit its cargo of dignitaries he couldn't help asking himself: is any of this real? Did that lollipop man speak a profound truth when he had a go at me while we were overground? It ought to have been the holiday that felt illusory, a memory not too distant in time but so remote from normal life as to be like a dream. Yet it was superficial Scotland that seemed authentic to him now, the Burrows he had been in all his life that felt insubstantial. The limousine arrived and Dave Vinsky leapt instinctively into action like the trained professional his social network profile said he was. In other words he snapped out of it.

Professor Vanguard Pym considered the possibility that Annie Thromnick had abseiled to the centre of the Earth using mainly her teeth. 'You're right it's impossible.'

'I did vomit, though. And it stayed floating in the air . . .'

'Like a glitterball above a dancefloor.'

'Not really.'

'It's a nicer image though.'

'Finally I got to my feet and it felt weird, not having any gravity, no up or down.'

'How about sideways?'

'I suppose I still had that.'

'Then why didn't you just turn yourself in that direction instead? Better than nothing, surely?'

'You had to be there, Professor. What with all the strange lights and the ball of vomit . . .'

'You mean glitterball.'

Phoebe came in eating a ham and cheese baguette. 'Are you still on about eyeballs?'

'Glitter,' the Professor corrected. 'It seems there's one at the centre of the Earth.'

Annie continued a story whose truth only Dave Vinsky might fathom, though he wasn't there, he was walking his Alsatian dog. 'I stumbled a bit,' she said, 'then realised I could walk along the side of the plughole which was no longer a wall but instead a floor.'

'Couldn't you propel yourself through the tube like the astroscots did?' Phoebe asked, but the Professor silenced her, not wishing to bring up the subject of the space station.

'I tried but it didn't work,' said Annie. 'The plughole had a kind of stickiness, I don't know how. Magnetism or something. I made my way along this glowing pipe until I realised that the colours weren't changing any more, the light was fading.'

'At this point was it mustard or lime?' the professor inquired.

'Mustard,' said Phoebe, who thought he was asking about her baguette.

'Then it went totally dark and the gravity switched itself back on. I had to grab for the sides and it was fifty-fifty whether

I ended up the right way round, otherwise I was going down head-first and I was finished.'

'So which was it?'

Dave Vinsky came home with the dog whose sad eyes followed him to the living room where Vinsky sat in the armchair and for the first time in his life thought, what if I ended it all? Would anyone even really care? The dog stood in front of him like she knew.

'We have to go back there,' Professor Vanguard Pym declared.

'How the blazes are you going to climb down the plughole?' Annie asked.

'What I mean is, you've got to go back there.'

But it had taken Annie a day and a half to climb out again, plus the half day she'd spent beforehand trying to figure out which way up she was. Annie was in no mood to repeat the experience. 'It's hell, professor.'

'That's a religious view, you're not allowed to express it in a public health facility.'

'I meant metaphorically.'

'Like squeezing your eyeballs?' Phoebe suggested.

'No, that was an analogy.'

Dave Vinsky got up from his armchair, took hold of the dog's collar and led her to the back door. The garden was a mess, Shehalagh had been on at him ever since they moved in, about getting rid of those big stalagmites she kept tripping over whenever she went to hang out the washing. Vinsky encouraged the dog to go into the garden, usually she liked it but the animal seemed reluctant this time, unwilling to part from her master. Eventually Dave just had to push the door closed on the poor mutt who whimpered for a bit then accepted exile, tail drooping and head hung low, going to mope beside the shed. Dave put on his coat, went to the front and out, walking briskly along the access passage towards his destination. He passed the Pre-Cambrian Experience, heard the distant sounds of fair-ground rides and pounding music and screaming, laughing people. Took him twenty minutes to get all the way along the fence, then a stretch of rubble with not another soul in sight, until eventually he reached the place he was aiming for, a ring of darkness surrounded by the empty cheerfulness of advertis-ing hoardings.

Dave Vinsky stood at the edge of the plughole, just like so many others had done before, and would do after him. We all have our moment, he told himself, then it's over and might as well not have happened. History's meant to be the thread of significance that makes everything worthwhile: the memory of your kids if you have any, or your friends or the people you loved, or who knows, maybe you do some little heroic thing that gets noticed, some special act that's worth mentioning over a pint. And history is vertical – being up to date, maybe going down in it. Life yearns for the horizontal Now. But the deeper you go, the smaller it gets. That's the wonder of it, Dave Vinsky thought, the wonder of anything, falling through nothing into nowhere. The Burrows have never existed, nor the Overland that claims ownership of it.

Professor Vanguard rolled in his sleep, woke and felt Phoebe's breath on his cheek. He thought he heard a noise outside, a dog perhaps? A scream?

Ian Seggie rises early and checks his diving suit. The guide at Mary King's Close puts on her seventeenth-century costume, ready for another day's imagined heritage. In his secret bunker, the Secretary of State presides over rehearsal for a make-believe war and for every pit village a new day's honest hardship begins. In a cave, Ninian prays.

Our forebears chose to dig.

New Paisley

Michael Gardiner

–You don't have much.

–They said not to.

–Ah, the guard says. First time underwater people sometimes overpack. This your first time in the US?

Vee nods. She feels grimy and dumpy and badly dressed and disoriented from being on the sea rails for two hours.

–This your first time in the Atlantic? But you can travel within England. To England, I mean.

–We can. She smiles to stop herself talking. You don't converse with border guards. He's muscular, handsome, over a hundred kilos. She watches him go through his documents.

Welcome to the US, he tells her.

And outside, in the enormous light and space, her hosts are waiting.

The name hadn't meant much to her: Philadelphia. The Liberty Bell. A virus from the film age. She'd looked through the publics but hadn't seen see much. She was lucky to have access to the publics at all. What kind of access would the general population have in Philadelphia. The generals.

And why had they wanted her, Vee Mac, a thirty-year-old public worker from a low-rise flat block in an unglamorous corner of Europe. She imagined the elites roaming across the blanks in their world, wandering around those dark continents.

Not that she'd hesitated. It was one thing to go to England, but to the other side of the Alliance, how often did that happen?

Probably they'd come into some funds. These colleges did, they came into these endowments, accrued interest. They used it to show diversity. They had to show they were in touch with visitors, with Europeans, with their own general population. Their generals. Their gens. The elites and the generals: how did people ever get used to this.

And did they even know what she did for a living. Filing claims for Renfrewshire council. It wasn't that she had any special skills. Did they even know what it meant, social security? Was she just a curiosity, was that what it was. But she wasn't going to be a zoo case, she was sure of that.

As it turns out, there's little staring. A sideways flicker from the elites, burning the skin like the high American sun. Then the quick glance away. The general population engaging full customer care, going about their tasks noiselessly. So it's true about the Alliance: the elites walking straight and absorbed in ever-moving news streams like they're in some other dimension, the generals trapped in dimensions they know too well.

Vee tries to waits it out, the shock, in the airy tree-lined apartment they give her on campus, lying alone half-awake like she has jetlag. She sometimes wanders around curiously in this warm sun. They tell her not to go beyond the campus perimeter fence into the reservations. But in the end it's staying on campus that causes the trouble.

For if it hadn't been for this mixture of progressive elites competing to be seen with the visitor, and the uniformed generals obediently listening to her talk, if it hadn't been for this, New Paisley might never have happened.

She finds that every half-formed idea melts away as soon as she enters the tall seminar room. The faculty hardly seem to notice, glancing up from their terminals to smile, suited and marble-featured. And how interested had they been really. Soon she abandons her notes and invites questions about the old Europe. Without college fees, how did they get the right people. Did everyone mill around together in the street all jumbled up. Were there residential areas with no fences and no protection. Why did her chunk of the island insist on leaving England, where the market worked. Were there always queues outside grocery stores. Did the successful really paid 100% tax.

And they've sedimented over decades, the questions. They're unanswerable and they keep coming back, like a worn-out joke. At least once a week she considers booking the seaway back to Europe and quitting. One quick apology then home to her friends and her flat.

And yet, the spring is warmer than any spring she's known. She's drawn along the wide pathways by the rustling of leaves and the whoosh of water exhausts. The boulevards full of careless elites flirting with blissed neotenic smiles. All around space and sky and unquestioned ease. She squeezes into the summer dresses they give her, and yet the fabric seems to melt round the body to fit her movements, drawing her squat proportions into the proportions of an elite. She walks in it like a second skin and feels part-evolved already. How easy it would be to get swept along.

And only sometimes does she realise, with sudden horror, that hours have passed without her noticing the generals at all. The generals are buried so deep in the background they're almost invisible. They cling to the walls like ivy, like their uniforms have been designed as camouflage. They stoop and glance around themselves rapidly, looking for undone jobs, looks of apology painted on. And they're different, already they're distinct. When you saw the gens, you couldn't pretend to yourself that that the division hadn't already started. And you could have given them the smart fabrics, remodelled their bones, fed them lines, and they'd never have passed for elites. The mutations had been building in the blood for generations. And the elites paid them no more attention than they did the squirrels on the lawns.

But Vee finds it hard not to speak to them. She speaks to the canteen servers, to the lawn assistants, to the cleaner who ghosts into her room. And the gens nod and suffer her talk, engaging full customer care.

But there's nothing like a conversation till she bumps into the general tagged JANE. Jane is wearing a lawn assistant uniform. She's walking through dusk looking ahead when she hits Vee shoulder-first and drops an armful of tools, then scrambles to pick them up. A small terminal lying amongst the tools. She presses it into her palm.

And from the start she's just slightly unlike other gens. Her movements concise, her eyes alert beyond the rapid movements. Hair tidy beneath the corporate cap, neck scrubbed under the soil. She may be fifteen, she may be twenty-five, she has come from outside the fence where these things would be known. She stands on the pathway making herself small. A couple of elites look up from where they're reclining on the lawn near a sprinkler.

–You got everything, Vee asks her.

–Nothing to have.

–The things you dropped.

Jane shakes her head quickly. Vee leans forward with her left shoulder, and Jane leans back with her right, like they have magnets in their elbows.

–You a part-time student?

Jane's dark skin reddens. My father was a lawn assistant. So was his father, and his father. Ma'am, I'm late.

–I just thought you might be part-time.

–All it is, sometimes I get a few minutes with the filters. No mischief. I like to find out things.

Her cheek is trembling. A general should never have the filters offered by a terminal like hers: and without the filters the skies are a deafening scream of information, nothing picked out at all. And this was the world the gens were supposed to live in, a world of noise and confusion. If you wanted filters, you had to pay college fees. And no one who looked like Jane looked paid college fees. She glances at the elites on the lawn.

–Never mind them, Vee says. What kinds of things? What kind of things do you like to find out?

–Ma'am, I have to clock in – Jane trails off, like the sentence explains itself. They're always clocking in and clocking out. They have no real work hours, the gens, they're always on call, always moving from one task to the next, always late before they start. And no pay, just funds enough to stay alive and keep a room in the reservations. She stands waiting to be dismissed.

–You're welcome to come to my talks. You know, I could use the advice.

–My father was a lawn assistant, and his father –

–My dad's job wasn't so hot. I don't think he minded. I mean, you'd be doing me a favour.

Jane looks, wide-eyed. God save the king, she says.

Vee catches the girl's soiled hand, and passes a list of times and places. Jane looks at the hand for a moment as if she's never been touched by one so white. Both sway slightly in the breeze, Jane's foot cocked to step back, as if paused on rewind. After a moment she takes back her hand, bows to show the top of a baseball cap, backs away, breaks into a run after a few steps.

'God save the king': she'd probably overheard it from the elites. Not much known about their corner of Europe. Europe they knew: Europe was the classics. But Scotland. The whole confusion went back to the break of the old kingdom. The press pretended not to notice: England was back in its ancient form and all was right with the world. Except it wasn't. In fact was it really England at all? Then came the Atlantic Alliance, and they said that America and the old kingdom shared values.

And then the first hints of the division. Vee knew that the division started with education. In England college fees once tripled in a single year. This decided who met, what knowledge was valuable, what networks formed and what babies were born. It was like taking a meat cleaver to the gene pool. From there, the subscription medicine, the stitch-up of the media, the gated communities. The division.

And it strikes Vee that in her whole year here she might never again converse with another general, not properly. Turn up to a student meeting: the bearing of the elites alone would chase her out of the room. Both sides had abandoned contact. They shared no expectations: they barely shared a language. The elites merely assuming their inheritance, as if by a law of nature. Like the ancient English phrase said, nature is always the guide.

–No, Frank tells her after the seminar – no, no, no. You're wrong. No. We find it just as shocking as you do. Frank skips in his stride to keep up as she walks through the sunlight at the wide edges of the seminar room, skips though his stride is longer than hers. –We know we need more, of the general population to enliven, to make up – He nods. She stops. He stands a head taller, eyebrows high, the sun behind him like a halo. His sculpted face searching for the right statement, and puzzled by having to search. Hair falling back in chiselled blond waves. Frank has explained how he's known a notorious faculty radical, for his willingness to extent beyond the boundaries. And with his lanky stance and his earnest expression, he looks, Vee thinks, not older than fifteen. He gazes at her like he's trying to unwrap a puzzling gift.

–I'm sure you'll find a way. For that's the one thing we need, he goes on, is the general population amongst us. He pronounces the term carefully to avoid the vulgar contraction. –But then, the parents have paid the fees, they have, you know, expectations.

He skips behind her towards the door, hardly noticing as he knocks over a kneeling young gen holding a washcloth. The gen silently rights himself without looking up, like it happens all day. Frank sees Vee's face and raises a hand to explain. She leaves before he asks her to stay for drinks. The faculty behind her watch her leave, with their stiff smiles and busy eyes, sipping detox. She strides to her airy apartment and closes the door tight, covers her face with a forearm and listens to the leaves tap on the panes.

All spring, the same questions and the same postures. The younger faculty radical and concerned, the older faculty wistful and sardonic. And the gens sinking further into the walls, falling from the face of humankind before her eyes. And she turns up to the talks, and she leaves before they ask her to stay, every week till the first of August.

It's on the first day of August that she finishes to find the girl tagged JANE waiting outside the tall seminar room. She's put on a cheap Lancashire of the kind the gens sometimes got, and she's leaning to peer around inside in tall seminar room. Vee pulls her in by the wrist.

–Sorry, Jane says, as she trips on the lintel.

–I never thought you'd come.

–But you're already finished.

An elderly faculty stops behind them as he sees her.

–I hope we can squeeze in another, Vee says.

The elderly faculty stares at Jane, and Jane stares at the paintings on the high walls, as if wondering how to dust them. Frank lays a hand on his shoulder, face fixed in a smile.

–Anything up? Vee asks him.

–No, he says. It's wonderful. Just wonderful.

But as Jane nods to all and begins to circulate Frank backs away, as if uncertain what she might do in this place. Jane is looking round the bowls of soft coloured balls set on ledges. Beautiful, bright, elite food: her digestive tract had been too small for some generations.

And the whole faculty part like this to let her pass as she circulates, until after a while a loose ring forms round her. A young female faculty with angular hair and a New England drawl is standing next to Vee, looking sideways at the windowpane as she speaks.

–You may have pulled this off.

–Pulled it off?

–You must know the faculty aren't used to this.

And the faculty with the angular hair smiles languidly and drifts off, cheekbones seeming to shimmer as she moves.

Jane looks back at Vee anxiously. Vee squeezes her wrist, turns to Frank. So what would we do?

–What would we do?

–To get Jane on a, on a course. Vee smiles too widely, showing her one chipped tooth.

–Jane, he says. Oh, the – name. Frank fingers the nametag. Onto a course. We should take it to the department. We certainly should. But Frank is lost to thought and detox. He nods very slowly, seeming to look through them both.

The flutter of interest in the gen lasts about an hour. Jane evaporates, barely noticed, back into the reservations beyond the high fence. Vee follows soon after, along the wide boulevards, hears the skip behind her. She slows to let him join. The air heavy and humid, the calm of dusk within gates.

–Sorry, he says, for being, distracted. I should make sure you get inside.

–Fine here, thanks.

He looks downwards along the bridge of his nose. –Better though.

She smiles, shakes her head. –Come if you're coming.

He nods as he enters and looks round the place. –I'm sorry they couldn't get you something more suitable.

She scowls while she pours. –They say you have a partner.

He pauses to think. –I'm married, if that's what you mean.

Marriage: she'd heard of it. When two persons contracted to have the same name. A merger of families. He was probably a Christian as well.

She passes a glass. Frank looks at the glass as if remembering something from a textbook. Red liquid: Europe. Bacchus. Desire.

–You could help.

He opens his arms. –Always.

–We could use a new location.

–Yes.

–I don't think the gens and the faculty will quite cut it in Dilke Hall.

Frank grimaces slightly at the term, clears his throat. Swallows some of the liquid and feels shaky. Alcohol.

–The Hall is wonderfully appointed.

He fixes his face to the taste as she looks. A face on which everything shows. A face which has never known worry.

–But somewhere more out of the way.

–You mean, so that the general population – can – come along.

–Your friend seemed to think it could be done.

Frank sighs. Kathryn. Kathryn with her shifting bones and her ill-disguised intrigues. –Of course, he says, it can be done –

–With everyone welcome.

–Though not in equal numbers, presumably, he laughs, then looks down as Vee shrugs. But could we really describe it as educational?

–Ah. She sips. Maybe what you call education is different from what we call it.

–Exactly, he says, uncertainly.

–And we might find out. After all, isn't that why I'm here?

Frank leans back and nods slowly. Was the revolution supposed to be this confusing? –The faculty wouldn't join us.

–Maybe not. But after all, what do the faculty offer? Of course, the students –

–Might be part of the problem, Frank says, raising a hand to his face and rubbing absentmindedly.

–But surely it troubles you, she takes a step towards him, someone like you. The way we're coming apart.

He turns his hip slightly. –Spend half my life countering it, he says, straightening up.

–The division.

He grimaces.

–As you say. He nods and raises the wine, but finds he can't drink any more.

So she waits. Summer deepens. The leaves at the windows turn dark green and brush on the glass. The gens want to clip them, but she tells to them to stop. The noise helps her sleep. The leaves and the deep electrical hum of insects. The heat just beyond the panes.

But nothing from Frank. He expects her to forget. They do: the elites often do. They mistake records for memories. Or he may be steeling himself to distance from her, despite his desire. They were all strategy, the elites.

Jane, though, Jane is a hit with the faculty radicals. She comes to the next talk, then the next. She brings a friend, then four. And the elites know they've been clandestinely supplied, for they have filters that no gen would ever have. And they find that discussion isn't as difficult as they'd feared. And Vee watches

Frank, drawn towards her and keeping himself from her, the dance intended to corner senior faculty to hide the fact that there are so many gens in Dilke Hall. By the next month, with the clouds deepening into thunder and gens asking Jane daily about the talks, Vee decides she will have to act for herself.

It takes her almost an hour to find the President's quarters. The President's quarters don't seem to correspond to any map, them seem, just blank. The President's quarters are a high-columned building in the central woods, porches and verandahs slung back like an old southern colonial mansion. The gen guards stare as she approaches. She shows them her appointment and they part to let her in.

The President gestures to a chair, reaches out his hand carefully across oak to shake hers, smiling wide as for a visiting dignitary. He pours detox and brings her wine without asking.

–I've waited to meet you.

–I don't mean to take up your time.

The President nods slowly, eyes exhausted from a morning gazing into terminals. He sips and his eyes relax and he looks younger, by ten, by fifteen years – impossible to tell when the elites never seem to decay, just redesign.

–You know,' he says, I've never met anyone from your country. Once there used to be a real connection.

–The division.

The President winces slightly at the word. –We send a number to Oxford every year. To England, I mean. England. Ah. The parents like it. Occasionally one of our brightest to Europe. But all those socialist governments –

Vee smiles. Even today the ruling party of England still described itself as socialist. It was like a tradition for them.

–But of course, the President says, that's why you're here. To help us understand.

–It's why I came today, she says. I'd like to try something more, more diverse.

–Yes. The President's eyes narrow as he regards her, gentle smile stuck on. The look of the visitor's face says high filters, says she's been up to something. Did she really want to learn about the ways of the Alliance at all? The thing is, speciation. The President sighs and pours more detox. –You do take that business very seriously in England. In Scotland. Sorry.

–As I understand it, she says, it's not just groups developing different cultures – it's the human body actually, splitting, into, you know, genotypes.

–You're very direct. The President raises a hand. It's all right. We expect it.

–I hadn't thought much about it before I came here. They say you can see groups in England but they aren't really, split. I mean, they have the old class system and it makes it seem that things are split. London of course: London's completely lost. A machine for making divisions. But London's not England, it just has their press. And England, sure they have the college fees and the subscription medicine and the gated communities and the huge underclasses, but there are parts of it that seem just like us. She pauses, realises she's been talking on. How often did you get to a president?

He waves his glass to tell her to go on.

–But here, here it's so – I asked a gen if she was a part-time student and she told me about her father's father. The two sides barely talk to one another. You can see it in the seminars –

–In the seminars.

Vee feels a chill on her skin. –Sometimes some of the generals come along. To the seminars. I hope you don't mind. Or it doesn't breach, the –

–You know, he says, I'm an idealist. But I wonder if it's possible to ever get rid of ethnic tensions completely. At least, in the Atlantic culture. I wonder if inequalities haven't always been there to some extent. I wonder if isn't like the English say, nature is always the guide –

Vee sips to slow herself down. A wine finer than she's ever tasted. In America.

–I understand, she says, what they say about the ancient similarities, the Oceanic culture, the Anglophone empire. But England is – the perception only really changed with the great financial shift. Their elites couldn't hold it together, they'd taken too much from the ones they represented. What you call the general population. It was only when the inequalities kicked in that the press started talking about the Atlantic Kingdom. And the politicians going on about meritocracy and incentive and reward. So when you send them to Oxford –

She feels herself spin slightly with the third glass of wine, feels the President watching her carefully. Wonders if anything else has been put in the drink. Places her feet flat on the floor.

–So you think we should set a more serious example?

–I think it'd be one way to look at it, Vee says.

The President nods, slow, tired. –Let me talk to the management, he says after a while. –I mean, he laughs, the real management. Maybe we can work something out. He glances towards his terminals without thinking, then back up. A wide smile dismisses her.

*

At the talk that week there are more gens than there are places to sit. The faculty stand uneasily, looking around themselves with foreboding. The gens are scrubbed from the water pumps in the reservations, uneasy in the tall seminar room.

–All these guests, Frank says.

–You said you wanted them.

He leans backwards, as if dodging a blow. He dismissed it quickly: living the ancient way, they sometimes came across as angry when they weren't. He knew this from basic anthropology. It was just that sometimes you hardly knew whether to feel chastened or braced. Paisley, he thinks. Scotland, Europe.

Kathryn is sitting next to them, wide-eyed on some hallucinogenic, gesturing at the full room. Her new bone modelling makes her look even more severe. –There are flecks, she whispers mischievously. Flecks in the President's records.

–I know, Vee says. I told him.

Kathryn raises an eyebrow. Frank raises a palm to his cheek.

–But he could close it all down.

–He could find us a place.

–He can spread it around, tell you you're doing great work, and make sure we're stopped. If we want to get anything done – we have to think of our records.

–Records, Vee says, shaking her head.

Kathryn giggles, staring at the shuffling gens. Vee turns sharply, but finds that Frank is holding her elbow. She feels a shaking in her arm.

–I'll do it, he says. Narrows his eyes. –You always knew, didn't you? Knew I'd do it. We'll call it research. We'll say it's for diversity.

–Well, Vee smiles, it is for diversity. But she feels the tremor: you can't stop it, the trepidation, when your record is everything and you are your record.

The building Frank finds for them is a turreted stone structure hidden by firs, almost pressing on the town railings. A hexagonal central chamber with a frescoed ceiling and radial alcoves where ancient hardcover books are stacked two metres high behind real glass. 'Seven feet,' Frank laughs, shrugging. An ancient plaque by the door, on which Vee can pick out a few letters: FERGU . . . HOLAR . . . SCOTI . . . EST 178.

She looks around. And what strikes her most is not that the building might be four hundred years old, but that those who built it might have made the same journey that she's made herself.

–It's not so luxurious, Kathryn says lazily. –I mean, by our standards. But Frank has warned her: you can tell by the glances. And Kathryn might be streaming proceedings straight to the President, but so might anyone else. It didn't matter: everything that happened everywhere was known. If something didn't stand out, it was because it was lost in the torrent. There was no spying any more, just patches of low interest.

They'd expected twenty generals to show up, maybe thirty. But for an unscheduled talk on a Sunday morning, under the faint ring of bells coming from the central campus, two hundred gens are sitting on the leather benches, in the aisles, leaning against the walls. Some are already in corporate uniforms, always on call, always late. Some in cheap Lancashire suits. Some are petrified, big-eyed: a shiver in the blood telling them they shouldn't be there. The generations inside them awaiting orders. Some are the age of the elites are when they go to high school, some are in that gen middle age that starts in the twenties. Their skin shades from honey to carob, their faces unmodelled. Seen together like this, you couldn't see them as anything but a new species. They press together for space on the ancient benches.

Vee tries to remember her own education. Five years in grey utility buildings. There was nothing to remember. But now she's already romanticising it: the way they all just expected it to happen. The way they knew it was free. How they learned about every subject, from teachers who bored them. But even here, amongst the whispering of the leaves and the distant bells and the shafts of morning light, she's already romanticising it. If she'd realised how precious it all was.

When she comes to herself she realises the audience are looking at the faculty. She glances around. No one moves. When she nods towards them, they avoid her eyes. After a while she steps up to the dais. Two hundred faces look up from the chamber.

She shouts into the chamber to try to cover the tremble in her voice. –So where can we start? Where, where can we start?

A murmur of bemusement, a long pause.

–Young lady. A man the age of Jane's father. For you to tell us.

–Sure, says a young operative suddenly, looking surprised to hear his own voice. No point us talking ourselves.

–We propose a course in radical thought, Kathryn says levelly from the side of the chamber.

–Maybe, Vee says, but I'd like to hear why you're all here.

The gens look. Look for a long time. Vee bites her lip. Ask the gens about their education: ask a zebra how to hunt lion.

–A better life, says a uniformed girl after a while.

–A better life. So some of you can compete amongst them. Or do you mean something else?

–Compete, a young gen echoes faintly, as if learning a line, looking at Vee for a moment for encouragement.

Vee feels the instructors bristle on either side. –Or perhaps, she says, there's something in the finding out. Why have things gone this way?

Silence. A faint nod here and there amongst the elders. A long pause, then Frank speaks. –Perhaps we can take a breather and rethink.

Vee feels herself sigh towards him. She nods in gratitude.

–And then split into three groups.

Three – Frank smiles across.

Vee shakes her head. –Into four groups.

And yet when they break, they're drawn as by some physical force to opposite alcoves. They talk in their groups like prison gangs. It made you wonder if the division could ever be slowed after all. And what FERGU . . . HOLAR . . . SCOTI . . . 178 would have made of this, the gens at one end shuffling around trying not to spread dust, the elites at the other, sipping detox and watching their backs.

And as they pass the decanter amongst the elites, Vee pours the detox and sips without thinking. And the moment it passes her tongue, there is an odd pause, then every gate in her brain seems to collapse. A flash of light and a rush of lightheadedness. The feel of the breeze between the columns on her skin, and a knowledge like all time opened up. And all at once she understands the gen slang word for what happens in this place of marble and oak: enlightenment.

–I hope they stay. She recognises the voice as her own. Realises she's speaking. She is gesturing towards the instructors, with their radical hopes and their trepidation.

–They'll come if you come, Jane says bravely. I mean it. You play him like this. She makes a fiddling gesture.

Vee hears a laugh and sees the girl's fingers held in her own, earthy and slightly curved. Face reddening. –I'm not so sure.

–You'll stay though. Jane looks up into her eyes.

–Stay: I've four weeks left on my visa. Do you know how long that took me to get?

–And then.

–And then, I can hardly stay without papers.

Jane rubs her nose and tin hoops jangle on her wrist. –As if these people have papers, she says. Gens have no papers. Half are illegals. And all the employers know. If we cheap and we keep to ourselves –

Vee rocks slightly on her feet, looking down at the gen's chestnut eyes. She looks at Jane, wonders if how she sees this pretty savage girl is how Frank sees her.

But there's already a murmur in the chamber where they're settling, some drawing their fingers across leather and brass studding, breathing hard like they've landed on a planet with thinner air. Vee looks at the assembly and with detox in her brain sees a future of two races, mutually reliant and mutually hateful, ripping the species apart. And would it matter if they did?

–And say the faculty went along. If I overstayed. What about funds?

–I don't mean nothing bad, Jane says. You get your chances like everyone else.

She is looking at Frank. She shivers slightly and struggles to put down a delicate glass with fingers too thick.

–And the authorities wouldn't chase up?

–No one chase up. The college don't need the attention. And say they moved on, the instructors.

Jane looks sideways at the three faculty fumbling before the settling audience.

–If not them, someone else. Always some with that, high thinking. The radicals.

Jane nods to show she's heard the phrase.

–Whole campus is full of places like this. Always some kind of project going on. No one asks. And they want it, really, the ladies and gentlemen. It's just that, what they have, you can't give that away. It's who they are.

–Speciation.

–Speciation.

And even as Jane's mouth forms around the word, her face seems to turn animal, to collapse before Vee's eyes. There is not much time left, she thinks, not much left.

–You could name it after your home town, Jane says.

Vee tilts with laughter, squeezes the thick gen fingers. –I suppose I could.

So she overstays. From somewhere a stipend appears, and she is left to the leaf-covered apartment. And although she expects him to see the joke, Frank has the words New Paisley sculpted into the stone above the entrance of the hall. It makes Vee smile and mutter every time she walks underneath.

But within a year, another two halls are sculpted the same. The faculty find them, these buildings, they hunt them out in the far campus forest, by the railings, where the smell of outdoor cooking from reservations competes with the chlorophyll. The younger radicals so keen now that Kathryn has to ask, all humble, to be retained on the staff. What staff? Vee wonders. And yet this whole architecture of fossilised structures has opened up from before the division. The same traces found on engravings and old books to be found in each.

And as they take them over, the ancient buildings, they find that they're left unimpeded. It's not that the authorities approve, it's that little attention is paid. For attention draws attention, and it's better to leave them alone. It's a minor scandal, but just that, a scandal. A fashion from Europe, gathering no influence where influence counts. There are few murmurs on the threat to freedom, but in much greater volume there are offers of help, from the American cities and the backwoods, from Canada, from the English radicals. And it's true that in England the arguments go right back: the press had talked of merit and desserts, but greater than them was the great populace pressing for the shared land they called the English way. The division, they said, was just some old empire habit the London press told the world. Nature is always the guide – but nature is always defined by the elites. And when you realise this, there could be a thousand villages like this in England, why not? There could even be a new Alliance between the countries of the old kingdom, an Anglo-Scottish Alliance. It was a thought.

So they visit from across the Atlantic from Yorkshire to California, they visit in number and still disinterest cloaks them in the American publics, concealing the village even as it gets stronger. Even from Europe they draw visitors, the elites queuing up now to make visa invitations. And the continentals shock gens and elites both with their candour and their pre-division habits, their casual assumptions of camaraderie. *Les gens sont les gens*, as the French phrase said.

And their technicians filter the village out to that world left behind, the world beyond the railings, the gated communities and the clandestinely supplied reservations, the sets of mutations separated by wire, the settlements human and not human, the lost gens walking stooped and heavy like trained pets.

In time, they find space to resettle some of the gens from the worst reservations. To the gens, the old unused dorms are fantastic luxury, with the beds and the spread-out furniture and everything hand-controlled. And life in a gated dorm: they're hardly sure if it's a blessing or a curse. They come and go through the railings, outwith the view of the elites. There are murmurs when the less cautious faculty describe the dorms as public housing. There's a rumour that the President is investigating a breach of some recent constitutional amendment, for what will they turn public next. But still they hear nothing.

In three years there is a whole infrastructure pressing against the railings. Beyond are the inner slums then the gated communities, the concentric pattern familiar throughout the Alliance. And they grow, built on endowments and dues from the gen unions which grow up in this place, as they find they can keep some funds of their own. They build housing, hydrogen tracks, a covered area for exchange – a black market, the elites call it. The filters get stronger and the detox is abundant, though the gens never take to it much. In the third year there are a thousand members. In the fifth they count their enrolment at more than ten thousand, including those rebellious young elites dropped by their families as soon as they make the jump. Soon enough the employers get nervous as gens' profiles begin to appear and they scramble for loopholes. Yet few of the gens even apply to that world. They build their lives here, a few even becoming instructors, standing in front of elites taking notes, and wondering if this is all real.

Vee is magnetic, a famous figure with her unmodelled bones and her Old Paisley tone. She learns the high filters and learns to organise. Frank files for divorce: the first divorce in the Pennsylvania elites for years, and it ruins him. It ruins him, but the gens don't see any change. And he waits, becoming less impatient for Vee rather than more, and appealing to her more for it. His eyes no longer follow the bridge of his nose. He no longer remodels his bones.

Vee never moves to the old plantation-style houses: the leaves concealing her apartment block a reminder of her first shocks. And she starts to see the pearled faces of the elites darken, the gens straightening up and becoming firmer of eye. This is what she sees, she sees it but you can never quite tell, for people look free when they talk free, and every campus is a bubble.

By the time a whole cycle had passed through the system, the newer faculty and the ambitious gens began to fumble with a statement, a public statement against the division. They throw some thoughts into the publics and find that most of them stick, for the elites can't be seen to object. They even exhibit a few paper agreements, there in the village, under the firs and the columns. Much bigger though is when they draft a great document they call a Declaration, feeling their way, filling the draft with outrageous statements on equality and autonomy, then putting it out without great hope. And yet the elites quietly agree to sign.

And the faculty tell Vee to invite the Scottish politicals, half-joking. For it was surely that splinter of England that first made this connection. They know the politicals can't come. They can send their support, but their ties with England – for politicians are politicans after all. Vee shrugs it off till she wakes from a dream of her leaving party when a handful of them took her paintballing before the pub. She tells the faculty her workmates are politicians: it's true, one of them stood for council in Eaglesham, although he came fourth. But Kathryn believes it, and by the next evening her father the senator has issued the visas.

In a week, eight of Vee's old workmates arrive, pear-shaped and bold and standing out under the canopy, where they're dressed as government officials while all parties sign this paper. All sign and shake hands. And they treat Vee like a lost sister, the Old Paisley eight, drinking alcohol in the sunshine and laughing, drinking alcohol and talking until the elites aren't sure what they're trying to say. After a while the elites begin to pick up the accents, their voices becoming louder, all raised to the sky like a slice of the old country has landed in the far Atlantic.

And the trees are left wild to grow for many Declaration Days to come, in the free state where the gens dress like elites, where they sit together in the stairwells of the ancient buildings and try to make sense of the past. The air in the high ceilings shakes with the music of days before the division. They drink freshwater or lemonade in the salons, canvas-covered and breezy, slatted chairs set round tree trunks. They say, even, that the two castes join, in the end, against every unwritten rule, and conceive in the old-fashioned way. Children passing in and out of the railings. No one mentions a thing. But in decades the skintones seem to coalesce, the stances seem to unbend, or to the ageing Vee they seem to. This is what she sees.

So they grow, tolerated and disregarded, cultish and unrealistic, under the trees and the columns and the canvas and the vast American skies. And they hear of the English villages, but here, they feel they've no influence outside this village, this new town, even for all their dreams of possible futures and their wonder. And they may be right and they may be wrong, but after all, they're only human. They're only humans facing the division, and what do you do.

The Sectarium

Gavin Inglis

This is not the story I was supposed to write.

I was visiting Edinburgh to cover the tenth anniversary of independence in Scotland. As a European journalist, they assigned me an escort. It was not that my hosts were trying to keep anything from me. Rather, they wanted me to see everything on their list: the firework display synchronised across ten ships in the Firth of Forth; the optimistic presentations from jovial councillors and leaders of local industry; the globally renowned fiddle player who had, supposedly by chance, dropped in to Sandy Bell's folk music bar to play on the very night we were there.

My particular escort was a poised hospitality graduate named Hazel, who wore her red hair in braids over an expensively tailored suit. She insisted on referring to me as 'Mr Neidhardt'. On the Friday evening I confided that I would like to skip the official dinner and dine somewhere less contrived. She offered to book one of Leith's famous Michelin-starred restaurants. But I asked for somewhere out of Edinburgh, somewhere close to ordinary Scots. That was how we ended up in Glasgow's Trongate, in a window booth of a late-night bistro, and how I saw the incident that would lead me to the story I did end up writing; to Scotland's biggest open secret – one of its great wonders, and perhaps its greatest shame.

It happened while we were waiting for dessert. I was toying with the last drops of my wine, looking out of the window, when I saw a boy approach. Hazel was watching the waiter, no doubt bored by the chore of escorting this polite but uninteresting Swiss correspondent night after night. The boy held something beneath his jacket.

I have reported from war zones. In such an environment, where a moment's inattention can be fatal, one becomes hyperattuned to the body language of concealment. This boy was drunk, very drunk; he staggered and weaved as he walked, yet he cut across the road with a determined stride and his head down.

Between the two carriageways stood a four-tiered planter. The boy climbed onto the bottom tier with some difficulty and braced his back against the structure. Then he reached into his jacket and brought out the object he had been hiding. It was a scarf: blue and white stripes, with a thin red line in the middle of each white band. The boy fumbled with its ends, then thrust his arms up in a V, drawing the scarf tight and horizontal above his head. He began to sing, thrusting it forward with each accent.

Hul-lo! Hul-lo! We are the Billy Boys!

The effect on Hazel was startling. Her head twisted towards the window and the drunken singer. Her mouth dropped open, and her eyes gave a telltale glance in my direction.

Hul-lo! Hul-lo! You'll know us by our noise.

I watched, fascinated. From the corner of my eye I saw a trim figure in black break through a group of passers-by and sprint towards the singer. He reached inside his own jacket.

'Please,' said Hazel. 'Don't . . .'

We're up to our knees in . . .

It happened so fast. For an instant there was a tiny red dot on the boy's chest, then a blue coruscating flash. He rocked back against the planter, then dropped to the pavement. As he trembled on the ground, the scarf slipped from his hands.

'You shouldn't have seen that, Mr Neidhardt,' said Hazel. 'I'm sorry you had to see that.'

An unmarked van blocked my view for about twenty seconds. When it moved off, the singer and the scarf had gone. Groups of spectators began to disperse, seemingly untouched by the incident. The assailant, the man in black, disappeared once more among them.

'What happened there?' I asked my escort. 'What was going on? Where will they take that boy?'

Her blue eyes held mine and she bit her lower lip. I could see how she must have looked as a young girl. 'I don't think I should talk about it,' she said.

My instinct was to rush from the restaurant, to interview the bystanders, but they were already drifting away, tired drinkers on their way home. I got the impression they had witnessed this scene many times before.

At that moment our dessert arrived. I had ordered *crème brûlée*. Hazel's ice cream was decorated with a miniature firework. We watched the tiny white sparks for a few awkward seconds before she took it and dropped it into her water glass.

Hazel did not appear at my breakfast table in the morning. I took only a single croissant. I had little appetite. The other journalists sat in small groups, chatting or checking their uplinks. I accepted a coffee from the waitress and lingered over its aroma, unwilling to return to the insulated, staged schedule.

A man approached my table. He had a round head and spectacles with square corners. He gazed at me and smiled. I disliked him immediately.

'Croissants,' he said. 'The hotel gets them from a small family bakery in Dalry.'

'They're very good.'

'Do you mind if I join you? I'm Stewart McAra. Chief Social Engineer on a project we call the Sectarium.'

A Social Engineer. Of course, that was why I disliked him. It is a global irony that the individuals who study, theorise and train hardest in the subtleties of community engagement and persuasion are faintly repulsive to their fellow humans. Perhaps this is a legacy from their body of knowledge: techniques which in the past were called pretexting, compliance, neuro-linguistic programming or even confidence tricks. The prospectuses talk of building stronger human structures through understanding our true selves; the reality is of graduates who look at others a little too intently and always seem slightly removed from any conversation. It is a young discipline.

This McAra was not interested in my breakfast. He wanted to make sure I did not write a negative story about the boy who was arrested.

I indicated the spare seat and he settled down. The waitress brought him coffee. He examined the sugar cubes closely before selecting one. His eyes were cool.

'I hear you visited Glasgow last night.'

'Yes.' The bare minimum, I decided.

'You saw a patient being brought in.'

'A patient? It looked like an arrest to me.'

'It's necessary to remove such people quickly and safely. Particularly in an environment where alcohol is a factor. The situation can escalate very quickly into violence.'

'So you prevent violence . . . using electrocution?'

'I can assure you, there was more to that situation than you understand. Did you recognise the song the young man was singing?'

'No.'

'It is called "The Billy Boys". It dates back more than a century. It was the anthem of a street gang of the same name. You may have heard of Glasgow's razor gangs. They fought over territory, and for the fun of it, but there was often a further component to their activities – an identification with Protestant or Catholic communities. The Billy Boys were a Protestant gang. They used to march through Catholic areas to provoke the residents. Their Catholic rivals were called the Norman Conks.'

'So the boy I saw was a member of this gang?'

McAra smiled. 'No. I doubt the Billy Boys as an organisation survived World War Two. Their song has remained popular because it's so adaptable. It doesn't have to be the Billy Boys. It can be the Craigy Boys or the Bishy Boys. Most place-names in Scotland are amenable to contraction and the addition of a Y.'

'So he was celebrating his district?'

'Not quite. You see, the fifth line of that song is "We're up to our knees in Fenian blood".'

'Fenian?'

'Originally an Irish republican. In Scotland it's simply a derogatory term for a Catholic.'

'He was shouting at Catholic passers-by?'

'No.' McAra smiled again. It was becoming insufferable. 'It's a hard thing to understand if you're not from Scotland.'

'And you are here to ask me not to write my story about this boy. Because I do not understand the situation. Instead you want me to write about fireworks and music and magnificent architecture.'

'On the contrary, I would like to make sure you get all the facts, so your story is accurate.'

'Very well.' I brought out my voice recorder and set it up. I hoped to intimidate the man, but he did not react; simply looked at me patiently.

'Interview with Stewart McAra, Chief Social Engineer on . . . what did you say it was called?'

'The Sectarium. A facility built in Irvine. A town in Ayrshire.'

'Mr McAra. Last night I observed a young man being incapacitated with an electrical device and abducted in a van. This appeared to be a reaction to him singing a song named "The Billy Boys". Please explain why he was assaulted in this way.'

McAra paused for a moment, calculating. 'Sectarian expression has been illegal in Scotland for eight years. There is a zero tolerance policy, except within the walls of our facility. The police have standing orders to remove any offenders to the Sectarium. The Trongate is something of a hot spot for offenders.'

'What constitutes sectarian expression in this case?'

'That's a good question. There are many proscribed songs and particular words.'

'You used the word "Fenian" earlier.'

'Had you been Catholic, and had I used it to refer to you, I would have been guilty of sectarian expression. Its use remains acceptable in a neutral discussion.'

'And what happens in your facility?'

'Education. Freedom of expression. Conflict resolution.'

'Punishment?'

McAra tilted his head to one side. 'We Scots have a peculiar relationship with punishment, Mr Neidhardt. Some say we, as individuals, spend too much time in self-chastisement. There's nobody in the Sectarium who doesn't want to be there.'

'In that case, why resort to electrocution?'

McAra gave me a long look. 'I can talk to you about this all day. But what do you writers say? Show, don't tell? Would you like to tour the facility? I'm proud of what we have created. And its activities are under-reported outside Scotland.'

The idea of spending an entire day with this man revolted me. The longer one spends around a social engineer, the more data they compile, watching reactions and habits, listening to inflections. Yet this story had a definite energy which had been lacking from my trip.

'Or, if you like, I'll leave you to your breakfast and you can return to the group. I believe the agenda today includes new developments in tartan weaving.'

I stared at the man.

The road signs for the Sectarium looked no different from those for golf clubs and museums, with white lettering on a brown background. What had I expected? My chauffeur drove me into Irvine on the Kilmarnock road, under a grim grey sky. I was distracted by the harbour to our right, where gulls wheeled and cried above red-hulled fishing boats. Then I turned my head and saw it.

The Sectarium was an immense silver dome, rising perhaps seven storeys, its faceted surface interrupted by two large black chimneys. It was surrounded by car parks. Figures walked between the vehicles, mostly men in their twenties or thirties.

The chauffeur stopped at a loop beside an elevated walkway. I thanked him and stepped out. The wind chilled my face, blowing in off the Firth of Clyde. As I approached the dome, McAra emerged and greeted me, his manner jovial. 'Let's get you in out of the cold,' he said.

The entrance felt like the gate to a military base, or a prison. Clear panels formed an isolation corridor watched by two men in black. Yellow-black hazard tape crossed the floor. A series of signs declared:

CAUTION: SECTARIAN EXPRESSION LEGAL
PAST THIS POINT.
VISITOR SAFETY GUARANTEED ON LEVELS 2–6.
VISITOR SAFETY NOT GUARANTEED ON LEVEL 1
OR BELOW.

A large 2 on the wall ahead suggested we were safe here. I shivered, and looked behind me at the exit.

CAUTION: SECTARIAN EXPRESSION ILLEGAL
PAST THIS POINT.
REMOVE ALL AFFILIATED CLOTHING.
THINK BEFORE YOU SPEAK.

A man in the exit channel was being detained by security. They pointed to a small triangle of green at the collar of his jacket, a glimpse of a jersey. He adjusted it and pulled the zip higher before leaving. I saw one of the security guards shake his head.

'The weekend is the best time to visit us,' said McAra. 'We have a full programme of activities and our tour will take in most of them. During the week we focus more on younger . . .'

'The boy who was arrested,' I said. 'I want to see him.'

Was that a flicker of irritation? 'Of course,' he said. 'He has an important decision to make later today. I've drawn up a schedule so that . . .'

'I want to see him now.'

He sighed. 'Of course. This way.'

The hall smelled of bleach and chlorine. We passed through a security door and up two flights of stairs. McAra led me into a cramped computer room with a bank of monitors. The operator was startled to see me. 'Take a break, Raymond,' said McAra. He settled into the vacated chair and began to navigate onscreen menus.

And suddenly, there he was, the 'Billy Boys' singer, viewed from above by a fisheye lens. He sat on a bed in what looked like a small but clean hotel room, knees drawn up to his chin. He wore a blue jersey. An elderly lady in a white coat was talking to him.

'We mix therapists throughout the day. It can be difficult to draw them out. There are some things they'll only say to other men. But to get to what they're actually feeling I find a grandmother figure generally works. Ruthless, I know.'

'What has he been saying?'

McAra called up a text file. As the woman on the screen spoke, her words became transcribed at the bottom. He scrolled back several pages and skimmed the text.

'He was silent for the first hour. Then there was more singing. Many times he repeated "No one likes us, we don't care." Then he made some attempt to engage the male therapist in anti-Catholic sentiment. That was followed by another extended silence. He is now talking about himself. He has been laid off from the DIY store where he worked. He has been depressed. He was seeing a girl last year, but they separated.'

'You have taken extreme measures to persuade this young man to talk about himself.'

'Perhaps. Please may we return to my schedule? I hope you can see I'm not hiding anything. And I have arranged the tour to lay out our programmes in a logical progression.'

I watched the boy. He seemed no happier than he had the previous night. But then, he had not simply been drunk. There had been a look about him, a kind of sluggish desperation. Was this the only route into therapy for a hot-blooded Scottish male?

I rose from the monitor and nodded my assent to McAra. We walked to an elevator.

'Excuse me if this question is patronising,' he said as the doors closed. 'Do you understand what we mean in Scotland when we refer to sectarianism?'

'Tensions between the Protestant and Catholic communities you mentioned, yes?'

'Yes. Do you have these troubles in Switzerland?'

'No. Well, not for hundreds of years. The Roman Catholic and the Reformed churches coexist peacefully. We have experienced more conflict about the building of minarets.'

'Really?'

'The Swiss people understand that things must change. But we are also very conservative in some ways.'

McAra led me along a curved corridor with a low sloping ceiling.

'We are now very high in the dome?' I asked him.

He gestured ahead to a large number 6 painted on the wall. 'This is the top level. Somewhere here is a maintenance access to the roof . . . but I won't be showing you that on a windy day.'

'There are no windows?'

'None on the exterior. That was specified in the original proposal.'

We approached a bank of small windows facing *into* the structure. 'Could I ask you to keep your voice down in this section? These are our classrooms.'

A green glow flickered from the windows. I peered in. A small group of boys, aged about nine or ten, watched a stylish animation of an army of kilted men walking down a misty hillside.

'The Jacobite Risings,' whispered McAra. 'One of a series. We also have Martin Luther, John Knox, Mary, Queen of Scots and so on. Created for us with as neutral a tone as possible. We have several edits of increasing depth and detail from which we select based on the child's age and intelligence. A teacher enters after the feature to lead a discussion. One teacher can handle two classes if the timing is correct.'

'The boys pay attention even in the absence of the teacher?'

'Girls, too, sometimes. Yes, they pay attention. They have certain inducements.'

'Why are these children even here?'

McAra gave me a hard look. 'Scotland has a law prohibiting sectarian expression. It applies to all ages. I have a duty of care and . . .'

'Children simply use words they hear! They don't always know what they mean!'

'I agree. That's why I have a duty of care and *education* towards them. It's the most important work we do. It changes lives.'

'You can't expect younger children to understand the intricacies of religious division.'

'No. If you'll come a little further I'll show you what we do instead.'

The next segment of the corridor held smaller banks of windows. In these rooms sat younger children, some playing with toys, some talking. In some rooms they wore blue or green T-shirts; in others, a neutral black.

'All we can really do for the younger kids is empathy training. At home they receive constant negative messages from parents and grandparents, but no contact with the subjects of that hatred. In here, we place them together with a rival child for extended periods.'

'You only observe?'

'We have some direct methods. The workers might ask each to explain exactly what it means to be a Protestant or a Catholic. What we generally find is that the children who are brought here cannot adequately define their own faith, although they are versed in defining the faults of the other.'

'Do you hold worship here? Inter-faith services?'

McAra grimaced. 'Hold that thought until later. We also run stronger empathy sessions. One of our most effective features a frightening adult who comes in and shouts at each child in turn. He or she uses a selection of carefully chosen abusive terms, the same for each child, and adds specific sectarian language against each. Normally both children will cry. The adult withdraws and we leave the children together. Sometimes they will isolate, but other times this will open a dialogue. It can have a very powerful bonding effect.'

'Does this empathy training prevent incidents like the one I saw last night?'

'Perhaps. But let me show you something else.'

I followed him back to the cramped monitor room.

'Exit cams please,' said McAra.

We switched to four separate views of the entrance bridge. Nothing happened for a couple of minutes. Then parents began to emerge, leading children towards the car parks.

'One session finished about five minutes ago. Here they are leaving . . . Follow this pair, will you Raymond?'

We zoomed in on a skinny man with a khaki jacket and a bright shock of red hair shaved at the sides. His son held his hand and walked with exaggerated steps, lifting up his legs like a cartoon animal. As they reached the end of the bridge, he turned his head and waved to another boy. It was one of those loose waves from the elbow that only children seem to use. His father noticed, and looked to see where the wave was directed.

Then he slapped his son, *hard*, on the side of the head.

'Yep,' said McAra.

The boy burst into tears and was hauled away, feet dragging across the grass, until the camera could follow them no further.

'Catholic family,' said McAra. 'The boy was waving at his empathy partner. A Protestant boy.'

I had to sit down.

'Sooner or later the father will cross the line and we'll bring him in. But by then it may be too late for the boy.'

'What is . . . the root of this hatred? Why is religion such a powerful force in Scotland?'

McAra and the operator traded a glance. McAra appeared to be trying not to smile. 'Come back tomorrow and I'll give you access to our library. No, in fact, come with me now. I'll show you something.'

We passed through another security door and into a quiet corridor on level 4. This one had better headroom and curved more gently. We came to a strange door. It was large, arched and made of mahogany. McAra extended a hand, indicating I should open it. I felt its weight as it moved.

Inside was a church.

Semi-circular pews ringed a dais upon which stood a simple wooden table bearing two candlesticks. Along the side of the table was engraved THIS DO IN REMEMBRANCE OF ME. Carpeted aisles extended through the pews like spokes, the scene tinted by what appeared to be daylight streaming through stained glass windows. There was a small organ to one side, a pulpit to the other, and seating for a congregation of about two hundred.

'It's beautiful,' I said.

'Yes.' McAra's voice was slow. 'Pat the cushion on one of the pews.'

'I'm sorry?'

'Tap the cushion with your hand. Just do it.'

I did it cautiously. A small cloud of dust rose around my fingers.

'It's never used any more,' McAra. 'It never really was. I keep it open because it offers comfort to the occasional bereaved relative. But I've cut the cleaning service. It was a waste of money.'

'People prefer to worship close to their homes.'

'No, Mr Neidhardt. Most of our users *do not* worship. On Sunday, they are in this dome, downstairs. Statistics on church attendance show a constant decline for at least the last fifty years. Nationally the figure is about 2.5%. The average age is 57. Behind there,' he gestured towards the pulpit, 'is a fully consecrated Catholic chapel. It is also beautiful, and also rarely used. We retain two chaplains, and that is all.'

'So why . . . why is all this necessary? Why do these religious differences matter?'

'For that I will have to refer you to the literature,' McAra said. He stepped towards me, eyes suddenly ablaze. 'But let me give you the short version. Famine in Ireland. Immigration to Scotland. Increased competition for industrial jobs. Discrimination. Different priorities in faith schools. Poverty and impotence. People denied a chance to fulfill their own potential and looking for something else to care about. Organisations of bigots. Violence around football matches. And old people for whom the perpetuation of old conflict is the most important thing.'

I stared at the man. His hands were bunched into fists.

'I'm sorry if I upset you,' I said.

He breathed and I watched the hands unwind. 'Not at all,' he said. 'My apologies. I'm trained to build positive communities and these are the frustrations of my job. Also, I am not looking forward to our next stop.' He checked his watch. 'First, would you care for a late lunch?'

The observation gallery on level 2 was fronted by what looked like a one-way mirror. McAra noticed my interest. 'That was a late addition to the structure,' he said. 'Originally, the moment you are about to witness happened with a public gallery. The audience could contribute suggestions. It became pointless. They only ever suggested one thing.'

Beneath us lay a long room. It had a single entrance door at one end and two exit archways at the other. About halfway along, the room became split by clear walls like those at the dome entrance. Bold symbols were painted on the floor: on one channel, a medical cross and a mortarboard; on the other, a warning triangle and a skull. Across the floor, beneath each archway, ran a yellow-black hazard stripe.

The entrance door slid open. Several things happened immediately. The mortarboard archway lit up in green. The skull archway lit up in blue. The room began to hum, the floor vibrating as if from an immense engine deep beneath. I felt it through the soles of my feet. And a woman's voice, bell-like and hypnotic, began to speak.

'Congratulations on completing your induction. Welcome to the decision chamber. You have five minutes to select an archway and exit the room. If you do not select an archway, you will be incapacitated and will have to repeat your induction tomorrow. The incapacitation process is unpleasant.'

A small figure stepped out from the entrance. It was the young man whose progress I had been following. His arms were folded. He still wore the shabby clothes I had seen him wearing last night.

'Select the green archway on your left if you wish to undertake a process of re-education. If you step through this archway, you will embark on a two-week programme of study and therapy. Upon its successful completion, you will be released back into the community. If you reoffend, you will be returned to the Sectarium. Each subsequent education programme is longer and more invasive.'

The boy advanced to where the room split. He tapped the partition, studied the symbols on the floor, and scratched his forearm.

'Select the blue archway on your right if you wish to join the gladiatorial programme of the Sectarium. If you step through this archway, you will permanently enlist in the Protestant combat staff. Your living conditions will be comfortable and you will benefit from courses in melee and unarmed fighting. You may receive visits from family and friends, but you will never be allowed to rejoin the community at large. This option carries a substantial risk of personal injury and premature death. Choose wisely.'

My mouth dropped open. McAra watched me for a moment, then turned his attention back to the boy.

'You now have three minutes to make your decision.'

'This is a psychological trick,' I said. 'Surely? Something you . . .'

McAra gave a tiny shake of the head.

The boy scratched again. He looked through the archways. I now saw there were stairs beyond each. The green ones led up to level 2. The blue ones led down to level 0.

'You now have two minutes to make your decision.'

He seemed to choose the green archway. He took a couple of steps. Then he came back.

'Come on,' I breathed.

Now I saw another object through the blue archway. A tight spotlight picked it out: a piece of folded orange fabric on a plinth, with purple and white detailing.

'You now have one minute to make your decision.'

I looked at McAra. His knuckles were white, pressed against the bench where we sat. I wondered if he – but the boy moved, danced almost, down the blue channel with the skull. He was singing again, pointing his fingers to the ceiling.

Hul-lo! Hul-lo! Hul-lo! Hul-lo!

As he passed over the hazard markings on the floor, I heard a pneumatic hiss. He turned to look back but a metal shutter slammed down, blocking him from our view. My last impression was of his face, filled with bravado which did not reach to his eyes. His blue scarf was wrapped in his fist. It looked like a child's security blanket.

'You did not expect that boy to make the decision he did,' I said to McAra.

'I hoped he wouldn't. But I'm not exactly surprised.'

'What percentage of them . . .'

'Of those who have stumbled in by accident? Hardly any. They look at the choice, turn pale, and run for the education exit. For Catholics, by the way, we switch the colours around. Selecting the colour associated with their rivals forces our patients to take a first step out of their comfort zone.'

We descended a service stair. We passed a large 1, then a 0. With some unease I remembered the note about visitor safety not being guaranteed. I heard a deep rumble through the fabric of the building, becoming louder as we walked.

'I take it they both lead to education programmes,' I said. 'It's simply a way to distinguish the degree of . . .' I tailed off as I saw the look on McAra's face.

He placed a hand on the back of my shoulder. It was a strange gesture. It did not seem patronising.

Then he opened the door.

The heat hit me first, then the smell: the stench of male sweat. The murmuring darkness ahead boiled with shouts and jeers. Stage lights swivelled on the ceiling.

McAra led me into a narrow black gallery with six or seven theatre seats. He unfolded one for me, but I simply stood and stared.

Beneath was a vast circular space. It must have occupied the bulk of the Sectarium dome, and dropped three storeys into the ground. Circular tiers of seating descended to a second, standing spectator area. Covered with graffiti, it was crammed with people. The audience was predominantly male, although I spotted a few women, particularly near the front.

Beneath, partitions created a sort of crossroads. A marching band was playing. The men wore black suits and ties, each with an orange sash like the one I had seen folded up earlier. I gathered they were Protestants. Some carried huge drums; some pipes and flutes; one a large banner; and most incongruous of all, each wore a bowler hat. One half of the spectators cheered them. The other half jeered. I now noticed that the spectator area was divided into two by fences. One piece of graffiti in the blue area read: KING BILLY 1960.

As the march reached the crossroads, a siren shrieked and two doors slid open, one on either side of the march. A column of men in black emerged from one side. I glimpsed green armbands – Catholics – before they charged the marchers.

The banner bearer, a pink-faced man, swung to meet the attack, twisting his banner to the horizontal. He yelled, 'YOU WILL NOT CROSS THE MARCH!' and slammed the banner pole into the faces of two assailants. The force of his blow knocked them back into the column. Its momentum flung them aside and it crashed into the marchers, buckling their formation. The fighting began. The orange marchers swung with flutes, pipes and the canes they used to beat the drums. The green invaders were unarmed but had the benefit of momentum and agility.

It was a brawl, simple and brutal. I saw fists flash; noses and eyes go bloody. They tore at each other's clothes; wrestled and spat. The weight of the Catholic incomers stretched the Protestant cordon to breaking point. Protestant spectators howled. Then suddenly two, three greens vaulted through a gap and sprinted for the exit. The Catholic crowd roared. The march tightened formation to restrain the others. A surge, and they were pushed back towards their entrance. The siren howled once more . . . and the event seemed to be over. The teams dispersed to their respective exits.

'Technically,' said McAra, 'the marchers lose if a single Catholic crosses the route. But in practice it's a good result if the formation maintains discipline. I'd call that one a draw with the decision going to the Prods.'

I looked at the man. My mouth was hanging open. 'What did I just see?'

'This,' said Dr McAra, 'is the Sectarium.'

I watched the partitions slowly roll back. A team of men in black-and-white striped jerseys began to clean the floor. It was littered with blood spatter, pieces of musical instruments and dented bowler hats. The audience yowled and jeered.

'You had better sit down,' McAra said. 'If they notice anyone in this viewing gallery they might throw things. The crowd is very unpredictable. Every now and then we weaken the fences between the spectator sections so they break under pressure. We let the spectators pound the hell out of each other for five minutes before we pump in the gas. Then we take them out in wheelbarrows.'

I sank onto a chair. 'People come to this for . . . entertainment? For their Saturday afternoon fun?'

'Why does it surprise you? Football fans clash all through Europe. Even in Switzerland, yes? Zürich and Basel? The antagonism is part of the experience even for those who don't want violence. Here we've allowed people to choose their own level of participation, while protecting the community at large.'

'Why is football so important here?'

McAra sighed. 'In Scotland? It just is. Watch.'

The arena was completely clear now. The cleaners folded back panels to reveal a synthetic red turf, and goalposts rose slowly from the ground at either end. There was room for an entire half-size pitch.

'They are going to play . . . football . . . after what I have just seen?'

'Our own variant.'

'Why is the turf . . .?' I let the question dry on my lips.

A pre-match warm-up video had begun, celebrating the teams of the past and their achievements. Glasgow Rangers. Hibernian. Heart of Midlothian. Glasgow Celtic.

'We still have Scottish football, of course,' said McAra, 'but the legislation was the end of affiliated teams.'

The air became electric. An inspirational quotation burned the wall above each arch as the teams entered. For the blues:

WHEREVER THE PAPIST BEAST SHOWS ITS HEAD
WE MUST CRUSH IT.

– John Cormack

For the greens:

SATAN HIMSELF CAN FAIRLY BE REGARDED AS
THE FIRST PROTESTANT OF ALL.

– Compton Mackenzie

The crowd rose and thundered their feet on the floor. I saw an old man scream himself hoarse. There were six players and a goalkeeper on each side, green and blue strips with white shorts. I thought I had been mistaken about the turf until I noticed the gleam from the fists of each player. They wore knuckle dusters on which were mounted a short convex blade.

'What are the rules?' I stammered.

'First to ten wins. No substitutions. Once you leave the pitch you can't return. Assault is illegal over the perimeter line.'

The kickoff moved fast. The greens took the ball towards the blue goal. An early shot hit the post, bounced back – and the shooter was sliced across the shoulders by a blue defender. I saw blood arc in the air. The wounded player grabbed for the wound, backing off. The blues took the ball on the rebound, and from just outside the penalty box, they scored. The

Protestant crowd leapt and howled. I felt the sound in the soles of my feet.

The shooter took advantage of the moment to pounce on the Catholic goalkeeper, blades flashing. Two defenders hauled him off and sliced his neck. A Catholic sweeper picked up the ball and made a run up the wing, only to be jumped by a Protestant midfielder. It became a lethal dance, each darting forward to snatch a kick of the ball, retreating from an opponent's attack. The blue player ducked beneath a swipe and hooked the ball away, pounding up the centre of the field while defenders duelled the men they were marking. A quick strike and it was 2–0. The crowd hooted. The shooter kept on running. And the Protestants in the audience were singing now, singing together. It was a melody I recognised from European games, 'You'll Never Walk Alone'.

Walk on, walk on, with hope in your hearts
But you'll ne-ver get . . . a . . . job.

It seemed to cue a pre-planned manoeuvre. Abruptly, the green players formed pairs and isolated single blue players, striking from both sides. The body count rose. A blue midfielder ran with the ball, shooting a third goal, unaware that his team were being carved into meat around him. As I saw a wounded Protestant scrabbling desperately towards the safe area under the shadow of two heavy-built greens, I had to look away. I heard a fourth and fifth goal for the blues, then no more. The song had changed.

They were eating ripe bananas when they saw our Fenian banners,
And the dirty orange bastards ran away.
They ran away, they ran away . . .

I looked over the edge of the gallery, not wanting to. Three blues and one green lay unmoving on the pitch. One had taken a huge cut to the stomach and wet guts trailed from the wound. Four blues had made it to safety. three of them with dark, drenched shirts. The greens prowled the pitch, scoring lazily and casting obscene gestures at their mutilated opponents.

Have you seen the handsome Hun?

No-ooo. No-ooo!

'Surely your government . . . they cannot endorse this?' I asked.

McAra sighed. 'They know what goes on but they don't take an interest. The Sectarium enforces the law. It makes a problem go away . . . and it's entirely self-funding. Why would they disturb it?'

'Self-funding?'

'Our season tickets are very expensive. But the bulk of our funding comes from overseas broadcast rights.'

'No.'

'Yes. We're consistently popular in the darknet charts. The Middle East in particular cannot get enough of our programming.'

'Get me out of here.'

'There's one more event to go . . .'

'I don't care. Get me out.' I stumbled to the door and pushed through into the cool corridor. I held the vomit back until, for some reason, I thought of my father taking me to a club football game when I was a boy. Then I brought up the lunch McAra had provided. Its remnants dripped down the wall.

'Sorry,' I whispered, wiping my mouth.

'No apology necessary.' He seemed embarrassed. 'Come back to the control room.'

I stared at my feet as we climbed. 'The boy I saw last night. He will end up in these games?'

'Yes. Probably the march to start with. He can stay there for a long time if he plays an instrument. There are many non-lethal contests too, even for the children. But as they get older . . .'

We arrived back among the monitors. The operator glanced at our faces and vacated the room.

McAra looked tired. 'The last game for this session is called "Up To Our Knees". It'll be on that monitor. There are about ten other games that rotate from week to week. My latest idea is something called "The Menace of the Irish Race to our Scottish Nationality". I think my best designs are behind me.'

I wanted to leave. I didn't know at that moment if I would write my story; if, actually, I would ever write another story at all. The sheer depths Scotland had constructed for herself left me sickened. But I had one question left. I looked at McAra.

'Why have you shown me all this? You don't need publicity from me if you are already selling your feeds. A mainstream story can only work against you. Why take the chance?'

He smiled. This time the pain was clear to see. 'Because, Mr Neidhardt, the Sectarium was never meant to be a container for this conflict. It was meant to be a *solution*. The actual figures for sectarian violence were much less than the public perceived. But politics is more concerned with perception than accuracy.

'By now, Scotland ought to be as revolted as you are. But Scots have accepted it. We have acclimatised. If the facility had to shut down, if the conflict spilled back onto the streets . . . that would feel like progress. Instead, it's kept in here. It's too easy. They call this one of Scotland's Seven Wonders. A world-class centre of conflict resolution. You tell me. Is it?'

I glanced at the monitors. Two men wrestled inside a transparent narrow box with triangular blades protruding from its interior. Strobe lighting caught them gouging, strangling, biting. Each was hurt, dark blood dripping from wounds on their back and shoulders. As I looked more closely, I saw them brace their feet on sodden bodies inert on the floor. A queue of combatants from each side waited to enter the box when their teammate fell.

There was no drain to take the blood away.

A Beginning

William Letford

There's movement by the loch. Scientists. Some days Ben can't decide who gets in his face the most, the tourists or the scientists, but the city needs them both. They're part of the system, the same as midges and bloated fish.

He turns away, wanders up the east bank, searching for a seat to enjoy the morning. Gilbert McMillan comes into sight, lounging on a stone bench.

He looks up. 'Hello, Ben.' Gilbert's a scientist, but he's no bloated fish. He's much sharper than that. He says, 'Take a seat.'

Ben considers walking on, but sits down beside him. Gilbert has one good eye, and one bad eye. His good eye, when it snares you, is like a drill. His bad eye is more like bad breath. Which one should you focus on?

'You're up early, Gilbert.'

'You know me, up with the sun.'

And that's no lie. When Gilbert was fourteen he covered his left eye with his hand, and used his right eye to watch a solar eclipse. He didn't protect himself, and the dim light from the eclipse fooled his pupil into dilating. When the doctors examined the fourteen-year-old Gilbert they found an arc of swelling on his retina. A perfect sickle. He lost seventy per cent of the sight in that eye and, perversely, fell in love with the sun. He's been studying it ever since.

Ben looks out over the loch. 'You should have a better tan.'

'Don't let the modern fad fool you. A tan is a surefire indicator of working class.'

During the course of the year, Ben and Gilbert's conversations had taken two forms. The first was born out of necessity. They were on the same course, a course that consisted of six students. Some form of profitable communication had to be developed. The second was one that Ben felt more comfortable with. The trading of insults.

Ben says, 'I'll wear that tan with pride then.'

'And that's the inverted snobbery that'll keep you exactly where you are.'

Ben moves his head slowly from side to side, taking in the view. 'Climbing the social ladder, Gilbert, is as useful as ramming a pole up your arse to see better at a concert. I'll just find some room and dance.'

Gilbert thinks about this, then leans back on the bench. 'It's a beautiful day, is it not?'

'It definitely is.' Keeping it cordial, Ben could handle that.

Gilbert sits forward, animated all of a sudden. 'Have you seen those sculptures on all the roundabouts in the Central Belt?'

Ben hadn't.

'My god, man, they're monstrous.'

'Who got the commission?'

'Obviously someone who's got an uncle on the council. You'll know the artist no doubt, he's a welder. They're metal. Probably took the same course as us, and lo and behold! a year later he thinks he's Rodin. Christ,' says Gilbert, leaning back again, 'outside Cumbernauld there's a giant woman with her metal mound out. I almost lost control of the car. '

Gilbert isn't a big man. Medium height, slim build, button nose. His only distinguishing feature is that blind eye. Ben has size to back him up, the security of a solid right hook, a clincher, so to speak. Maybe no one's hit Gilbert before. Maybe Gilbert McMillan has failed to develop a fear of physical violence. Maybe Ben should sort that out right now. Ben stares at Gilbert's jaw then lets the fantasy trail off. 'Why does it bother you?' says Ben. 'What difference does it make what I want to do?'

Gilbert gestures at the loch with a sweep of his arm. 'Look at this place,' he says, and manages to time the gesture with the sun cresting the hills behind them. 'There isn't a city in the world like this. Right now, at this moment in time, this is the place to be. How did you manage to get on Moira McPake's course? Surely someone with something better to teach me could've been given your place.'

Ben stands up and takes a few steps forward. People are up and about, on the loch, beginning their day, boats cutting back and forth, and he can hear bird noise from the Long Island. No rush of cars on the roads behind. That's what makes the difference. When he turns round Gilbert is leaning back, arms spread over the top of the bench like wings.

Ben says, 'You don't care, do you? And why would you?' The sun is rising behind Gilbert. 'What have I got that you want, Gilbert? You're off to change the world. It amuses me that I make you angry.'

'Do I look angry?'

'No, but you are.'

Gilbert says, 'What's the bench that I'm sitting on made of?'

Ben tilts his head. 'Sandstone.'

'Where does it come from?'

'Cairnryan Quarry.'

'This is the material you like to work with?'

'What's your point?'

'Look behind me.'

Ben has to shade his eyes.

'If there's a god on this earth, there it is. That's the material I work with.'

Ben reaches into his back pocket and pulls out his sunglasses. He likes his sunglasses. His father bought them in the early eighties and passed them down, like a family heirloom. He puts them on and says, 'That's better.'

Gilbert continues. 'You know the architect I'm working with. From now on it'll be sun first, then sky, then trees. Cement and steel will be last. What are your plans, Ben Thomson? Should I hold my breath?'

'I'll keep chipping away.'

'Moira must've seen something in you.'

'Ask her, you've got your meeting today.'

'What have you and Agnes been teaching each other? Tell me, I'm interested. Has it been six months of one dry stone dyke?'

Agnes calls Gilbert 'the troglodyte'. Ben laughs. 'You're an unhappy man.'

Gilbert stands up. 'I'm unhappy because things need done.'

'Your idea of what needs done is different to mine.'

'It shouldn't be.' He walks towards Ben. Walks past him, looks out over the water to the islands. 'Think bigger, Ben.

Stretch yourself, how do you think this was called into existence.'

All of the buildings on the Island of Women have living roofs. Even this close it's not easy to tell the difference between landscape and living quarters. Ben says, 'You've got a lot to get through, maybe you should get a move on.'

Gilbert claps Ben on the shoulder. The sudden contact makes Ben jump. 'I'll keep an eye out for you, Ben Thomson. I'll study the roundabouts as I'm passing. You never know.' Gilbert turns inland and sticks his hand in the air as he walks away. The movement is dismissive.

Ben thinks, So much for enjoying the morning.

The Island of Women is not, as the name would suggest, inhabited solely by women, although sometimes Agnes wishes it was. Especially today. Six students, six lecturers. Halfway through the year the lecturer has to choose a student whom they believe can teach them something. The next six months is spent in partnership. She'd chosen Ben Thomson. No one else would have him. An artist could bring something creative out of him. He worked with stone. It fitted. So they said.

Agnes draws breath and settles herself. Last day of the course. One final meeting. Damn it, boredom had driven her to it. The complications and stress had certainly alleviated the boredom. Lesson learned. Thanks, Ben. From the summit of the Wee Hill Agnes can see all the major islands of the loch. She can see people on the south east shore of the Round Island. So many people interested in what's going on. So many tests. The whole world waiting to see. Yew Tree Island just beyond the Island of Goats, the first Water Scraper beyond that, and all the colours of June tumbling towards the loch from Ben Lomond in the east, and Ben Vorlich in the west. Another breath. Okay.

His studio space is beside the old graveyard. When work began thirty years ago they decided not to move the well rested bodies. Ben likes the gravestones. She found him once, lying on his back, directly above a Macgregor. When she asked him what he was doing, he said, 'Never so alive as when I'm down beside the beating hearts of insects, never so alive, never so aware of death.' She'd slept with him that night. Drink fuelled, of course. She'd thought there was something to him then. Something strange. She likes people that are off kilter. She likes people that are off kilter because normal doesn't exist. People that tie themselves to normality are tortured. But Ben Thomson doesn't just work with stone. He is stone. If there was something strange about him she couldn't find it. She should have ended it weeks ago but working together would've been a nightmare. More hassle than it was worth. No, she'd made the right decision. Wait till the course was finished. Wait till today.

She can hear him before she pushes open the door, sawing sandstone. Grind and swish. He loves the physical stuff. Give him something to lift and he's in his element. He's kicked his stool to one side so he can stand over the bench. The floor's covered in sand. He's sweating. A chunk of stone drops into his left hand and he turns round. She can smell the heat that's been created from the friction of the blade. He smiles at her. And she gets a glimpse of what's behind him on the bench.

'What's this?' She asks, striding forward.

He smiles wider. 'That's the inside of Gilbert McMillan's blind eye.'

'Where did you get this stone?'

'From a friend that works in Locharbriggs.'

The sandstone has a beautiful blood red slash of iron oxide. Agnes traces the colour. The way it spreads through the soft golden grain is wonderful. Ben has used the movement to dictate the sculpture.

'Look,' he says, and shows her the chunk that's dropped into his left hand. She takes it from him. Cradles it. It's heavy. The pattern spreads from the middle, from a rough circle of solid colour to thin spidery traces that travel outwards. 'I wish I could get inside the stone to see the pattern in three dimensions.'

She hands him back the cut. His tools are laid out neatly on the bench. Broken pieces of coloured glass, a bread knife, sandpaper, a palm-sized chunk of marble that he uses to smooth down, and that hacksaw. This is the one patch of neatness. Everything else in the studio is haphazard. There's a mattress in the corner. 'You've started sleeping in here?'

'Sometimes.'

'Good.' She turns her attention back to the sculpture. She can feel him looming over her left shoulder so she says, 'Put the kettle on then.' It's obvious he knows how good the sculpture is. His heart's racing and it's not just from the exertion of sawing through the sandstone. Positivity is rushing off him. It's filling the studio. Shit, is there ever an appropriate time. Agnes leans against the bench and watches him for a moment. He bends down to open the small fridge then stands up and looks at her.

'No milk.'

She can see into the fridge. It's filled with beer. 'Black'll be fine.' Why was he on the course in the first place? The only thing separating students from lecturers is the name. The six lecturers had to choose who would pair up with whom for the final six months, but everyone, so-called students and so-called lecturers, were considered brilliant in whichever field they'd chosen to work in. And here was Ben. When she'd heard there was a stonemason on the course she'd expected a modern-day Palladio. Ben Thomson wasn't Palladio. Agnes catches sight of some stone peeking out from behind the cans of beer. 'Why have you got a sculpture in the fridge?'

Ben answers while pouring water into each mug. 'Stone's different in winter. I wanted cold stone.'

Agnes had bumped into Moira in a restaurant in Fort William not long before the course began. She asked her why she'd started it in the first place. Moira had said she wanted to smash people together to see what happened. Agnes had come to the conclusion that Ben was indivisible. But then there was this sculpture. She looks at it again. There are human faces over it. Whichever way you turn it there's a face, some discreet, some pronounced, but every one of them has the deep red of the iron oxide incorporated into its features. The stone is twisting upwards, like a strand of DNA.

Agnes says, 'The inside of Gilbert's eye looks very interesting.'

Ben hands her the mug of tea then touches the sculpture. 'When it's finished I want to recreate it, much bigger, and put it bang in the middle of a roundabout just outside Cumbernauld.'

What a bovine thought, but Agnes keeps her opinion to herself. 'Good,' she says, 'it's great to have clear goals.' She had liked his broad shoulders at first, but eventually she realised he took up too much room on the sofa. Lying with her head against his chest would give her a crick in the neck. She had made a mental note. If you're going to spend too much time with someone make sure they're a small person. They take up less room in the corner of your eye. She takes a sip of tea. 'When's your meeting with Moira?'

'I've got a couple of hours.'

'Nervous?'

He takes a drink and slurps it down. 'No.'

He should be, and not just about the meeting. Thirty-two years old and trying to carve a living as an artist without ever having been to art school. He'll be whipped with the word 'amateur' for the rest of his life. 'We don't really need to talk about the course, we've talked it to death already. You know how I feel. You've got talent. It's rough. But you'll be fine. Keep going and you can achieve whatever you want.'

Ben's absently nodding his head. He puts down his tea.

Agnes takes another drink, slowly this time. Because there's that silence. The one she knows she has to fill. She just has to open her mouth and do it.

'Listen,' says Ben, and breaks the moment, 'we shouldn't see each other any more.'

Agnes coughs into her cup.

Ben steps towards her. His big calloused hands are trying to take the cup from her. She coughs again and bats his hands away. She puts the mug down on the bench and wipes tea from her mouth.

Ben takes a couple of steps back. He says, 'I'm sorry you're upset.'

Agnes shows him an open palm. She clears her throat. 'I'm not upset. '

'Okay,' says Ben, 'I know.'

'I'm not upset,' says Agnes.

Ben says. 'It's best just to get these things out of the way.'

'Wait a minute,' she says. 'You've been glued to me for the last four months.'

Ben shrugs. 'Think about how difficult it would've been to work with each other.'

Agnes is aghast. He's standing there, cold as the stone in the fridge.

'Look,' he says, 'these things are hard to take but you've got to hold yourself together.'

'Hold myself together. Who are you to reject me?' A rush of anger vents itself. 'Look what I've taught you.' She points at the sculpture on the bench. 'What about that?'

'You're right. I'm sorry. I never thought you'd react like this.'

Agnes says very quietly, 'Why are you even on this course?'

Ben rolls his head back. 'Surely I don't have to go through that again.'

Agnes spits the word, 'Amateur,' and slams the door behind her. Fragments of sandstone fall from the bench.

The islands are connected, though you would never know it to look at them. There's no fanfare as you drop below water level, no bells, no whistles. But there's still a rush. Ben never fails to appreciate it. Moira's meeting room is on the Island of Goats, between Long Island and Yew Tree Island. Quite a walk. Enough time for him to have a good think about Agnes. Movement helps his thought process. Working his body means working his mind. For her, everything has potential. She lives as if she's on fire. Drawing energy from whatever happens to be next to her. Anyone standing too close for too long would be left brittle and burned out. Good while it lasted, better to be away.

He eventually emerges on the southern shore. The outer edge of the island is mostly Scots pine, inland there's oak and rowan, and everywhere is a thick carpet of blaeberries. Moira's building is close to the remains of a jetty that was formed by large boulders. One whole wall of the front room is really a window punctuated by a door. He doesn't knock. No need. The receptionist, strangely, has no desk. To the left are two sofas, a flat screen television and a coffee table. The receptionist is lounging on one of the sofas with her legs tucked up beneath her. There's a laptop and a pile of papers on the coffee table, but she doesn't consult them. She smiles. 'Ben Thomson, take a seat.'

The receptionist is Moira's granddaughter. Nepotism is something Moira McPake has never felt the need to hide.

Ben returns the smile as he's sitting down. 'Cushy job this.'

'For the summer it is, then I'm off to Venice. Moira's got lots going on over there.'

'All downhill then, you have my commiserations.'

With her hand on her heart she says, 'We try to enjoy life in spite of ourselves. My name's Ella.'

Ella has jet black hair, bright blue eyes and a jagged McPake nose. Ben leans forwards to take her hand. Her grip is firm without being ridiculous. He envies her. Not in a negative way. He appreciates her life would be a good one. Ben sits back. The rest of the room is a shrine to the project: schematics on the walls, architectural drawings of a Water Scraper, an artistic impression of a Hydro Sphere and some pictures of a young Moira standing on the shores of the loch near Balmaha.

Sometime in the seventies, Ben would guess. At the opposite end from where they're sitting is a scale model of the loch, minus the water.

Ella is looking at Ben, closely, as if she's making judgements. Ben looks back at her. She drags her eyes back to the television, not because she feels compelled to, because it suits her. Confident for a teenager. The blood runs strong there right enough.

Something flashes up on the laptop. Ella strikes return. She says, 'My grandmother's ready for you.'

The bookshelves covering one wall are at shoulder height. Moira is replacing a book. This room has a desk Abraham Lincoln would be proud of. Moira leans heavily on her walking stick as she struggles towards it. There's a touch of anger in the way she huffs and puffs, it makes Ben feel uncomfortable. She waves Ben to come over, to the chair opposite, and sits herself down with a sigh. The legs of the desk, it seems, have been amputated. Moira is a small woman, probably grown smaller with age, and the desk has been fashioned to suit her size. When Ben sits down he feels ungainly.

'I used to believe,' says Moira, 'I would grow old gracefully. I never managed it. I have, however, managed to grow old.'

Ben doesn't know what to say to that, so he says nothing. Those bright blue eyes she's given her granddaughter are burning away. She lets the silence stretch. Ben remains mute and misshapen. He has the urge to cross his legs. He never crosses his legs.

'I heard you were talking to Gilbert McMillan early this morning.'

'I was,' replies Ben, keeping his tone light.

'He's very clever,' says Moira.

'He is,' replies Ben, without altering his tone.

'And how is Agnes?'

Now Ben knows he's being toyed with. 'Agnes is, good.'

A rising of the left eyebrow, perhaps the possibility of a smile. She composes herself.

Ben really doesn't know how this is supposed to go. No qualification at the end of Moira McPake's course, just an interview, where Moira tells you whether you've passed or failed. She tells no one else, and doesn't record the result anywhere. All you walk away with is knowledge. This was a selling point for Ben. Now that he's here though, he doesn't feel quite as comfortable with it. What he feels, in fact, is that Moira McPake may be enjoying herself.

Moira looks down at her shoulder and picks a tiny speck of white fluff from her pullover. She holds the piece of fluff between thumb and finger. 'You can see this.'

Ben can, just. He nods in agreement.

'You can see this because the sun is here, in this room. It is present. Always. We are constantly connected to it. Gilbert's one of those that'll help us understand the subtle way it affects life.' She flicks the white speck from her fingers. 'He is such a wanker though, why is that?'

No sign that she's joking, just a steady patient gaze. Moira's wrinkles are at one with her face. This must be her natural state, the inquisitor waiting for an answer, but the question is rhetorical, surely. Ben remains mute.

Moira still has a hold of her walking stick. She lets it rest against the table. The handle is a clenched fist. She struck someone over the head with that fist once, charged with assault at the age of sixty-five. Ben's glad she answers her own question. 'He's taken on the sun, has the scar to prove it. He thinks he's a warrior. He doesn't want to understand the sun, he wants to beat it. You don't like him, do you?'

'He's not a likeable person.'

'You don't have to like someone to learn from them. What about Agnes?'

'Are these questions part of the interview?'

Moira makes a point of deliberating, considering the options. 'Yes, they are.'

'She's a great artist.'

Moira waits.

'What else do you want to know?'

'You've spent the last six months working with her.'

'We had a relationship, it complicated things.'

'Of course it did. It does, however, mean you're far more qualified to answer the question.' Moira takes a mobile from her pocket and touches the screen. The office door opens and Ella pops her head in. Moira says, 'Tea,' and the door closes. She leaves the mobile on the desk. 'Nomadic people would light a fire whenever they stopped, even when there was no immediate need. The fire gave them a sense of home. Something to gather round. Something to fix their memories against. Tea has the same effect for me. So,' she says, 'continue.'

'Listen,' says Ben, 'Agnes is lovely.'

'Yes, yes, a kaleidoscope of butterflies we all know but what has she taught you?'

'I enjoyed her company. She has a unique way of seeing the world. That's all I want to say.' Ben stands up and walks to the bookshelves. It feels better to be on his feet. He wonders what book Moira was replacing when he walked in. He steps towards that area and narrows the choice down to three. *Highland Cities and their Impact on Worldwide Culture, Scotland and its Bilingual Heritage* and *A History of Independence*.

Ella comes into the room carrying a tray. She's very careful as she sets it down on the table. Ben takes his seat again. Ella begins to pour from the teapot and Ben says, 'I'll get that.'

'Let her do it,' says Moira. 'I have to keep her busy somehow. She can work her ticket like everybody else.'

Ben shifts in his seat and tries to make more room for Ella to pour the tea.

Moira says, 'You see, Ella, there's a man who doesn't feel comfortable being served. A dying breed. Okay, that'll do then. Get back and watch the TV before you give yourself a hernia.' She pours for herself. Ella closes the door and Moira says, 'I should probably tell you right now that you've failed the course.'

Ben blinks at the cup in front of him. Moira taps the spoon against the rim of her cup then sits back. He feels misshapen again. Should he ask why? Should he walk out?

'You didn't give anything, Ben. Everyone else that teamed up forged some sort of partnership, made plans to work towards something that could count. Gilbert and Agnes were very vocal about your apathy, and I have to agree. Look over there, Ben.' She nods at the far wall.

Ben twists in his seat, there's a painting hung on the wall. Crofters being forced out of their homes, pushed to the water's edge, but they're pushing back, their heels are dug in. The painting's called *The Beginning*. Ben's seen it before. There are prints of it on the wall of every history class.

Moira says, 'I often wonder what would have happened if the Clearances had been successful. What would our Highlands have become?' She holds up her cup of tea. 'Our country is what we gather round, what we fix our memories against. This course wants to produce people that can work the land.'

Ben's waiting for more, some other assessment, some other question so he can redeem himself.

Moira says, 'Good luck.'

And despite himself, Ben says, 'Thanks.' Then leaves the room. Ella looks at Ben as he walks past. He gets the feeling that she knew. He says, 'Enjoy Venice,' and closes the door behind him. The sun has fallen lower in the sky. So many beautiful colours of blue. The thing about the colour blue, though, is it's always out of reach. He looks down at his hands. He can work the land. What was he doing on this course in the first place? Waiting for people he hardly knew to tell him he could do something he knew he was capable of anyway. What had he failed? A sensation rises up. If she had told him he had passed what difference would it have made? Who actually decides? He looks back briefly and catches Moira standing behind that big window, leaning heavily on her walking stick, watching him being pushed towards the water's edge.

Glasgow Flourishing

Maggie Mellon

The Clyde rolls into Glasgow from its source in the hills to the south east, tracing lazy loops as it flows under road, rail and foot bridges and motorway flyovers, through into the dense heart of the city, then broadening out towards the Firth of Clyde and the sea. The city was founded here on this river. It is surprising how much green there is in Glasgow.

In 2024, the traveller entering Glasgow from any direction will find that food is being grown everywhere. The whole city is growing, harvesting, cooking or trading food: food to be eaten, sold or swapped for other life necessities and luxuries.

On windowsills, in communal back greens, in private gardens, in cans and tubs on the balconies of high flats, on thousands of allotments, everywhere there is earth, there is a plant. The ground around high flats, on wasteland, the grasslands next to now silent motorways, have all become urban growing grounds tended by families, individuals and small businesses. Every back green and street corner has its communal compost heap.

And the green city rewards its workers with potatoes, leeks, rosemary, thyme, carrots, onions, garlic, brambles, parsley, sage, turnip, apples and pears, beetroots, blackcurrants, strawberries and raspberries, barley, oats, milk, honey, cheese – all produced from Glasgow's land by Glasgow's people.

Folk who only knew chips, pies, burgers, pan loaves and sugar-stuffed sweeties and puddings now dine on broth, leek and potato soup, baked and mashed tatties, tomatoes, lettuce, onions, bran bread, oatcakes, flapjacks, crowdie, bramble jam, cherry pie, rhubarb crumble, stewed apple and yoghurt.

Cows, sheep and goats graze on Glasgow Green and in Queen's Park, King's Park, in Possil Park, Kelvingrove Park, and they are milked in dairies in Maryhill, Partick and Pollock. Byres Road has a byre again. Fresh eggs are collected from free-range hens in runs protected from foxes and other predators. Beehives, tended and sheltered from harm, provide wildflower and clover-scented honey.

Cooperatives have sprung up everywhere organising not just the growing but the cooking and distribution of food. Glasgow's produce is sold at markets in every quarter of the city. Produce can be bought or swapped for food, fish from Oban or Ardrossan, bags of flour and oats, vouchers for clothes, or for other goods made in or brought into the city, from surrounding farms and sometimes from further afield.

Cafés, fine dining restaurants, takeaways and soup kitchens all base their menus on what is grown in season or what is preserved. School kitchens are provided with vegetables and fruit for free, and grow their own, so that a free school dinner is served to every child every day of the week, and to other folk in need of a good meal too.

Out of school, children play and work on the allotments alongside dads and mums who have something to put on the table even if no paid work is available. Teenagers are allotted their own allotments. Men who have had no work for years, if ever, compare the size of their carrots and the crafting of their hutties built from old doors and plastic sheeting, where often they spend the afternoons, tending their tatties, and brewing tea.

Glasgow has flourished.

You will have heard a lot of claims about how it happened. A lot of people insist that they were responsible for the saving of Glasgow. It was the Greens. It was the SNP. It was the guerrilla gardeners, Sew and Grow Everywhere or the Allotment Bandits. It was the Health Board, the economic regeneration people, the social entrepreneurs. It was the experts, or it was the amateurs. Young people claim it. Older people claim it. Women claim it. The Brownies, the Guides and the Scouts have claimed it. The council claimed it. The Scottish Parliament claimed it. The Scottish government claimed it. The police claimed it. Celtic and Rangers both claimed it. All the churches had a hand in it apparently. What is the truth? How did it happen? 'Who cares?' some folk say. 'It happened.' But that is not helpful. You want to know what it took, how it came about, what helped and what hindered.

We were not making our daily bread. There was no work. Money was not safe in the bank. The supermarket shelves could be full or they could be empty but everything was expensive. And there was the land everywhere, in and out of the city. Land for growing, unused, neglected, and who was to stop us taking it?

We woke up and realised that the future was in our own hands. And the roots, the seeds, the mulch of what happened are so particular to us, so part of us, that all we can do is tell you our story, all our stories, and you can see if this explains our flourishing, and how your city might flourish too.

*

In Easterhouse children and adults are having dinner in the open, in the field between a school and a community centre. Fruit trees and trellises provide shade and shelter for tables and benches. A field kitchen made of wood and tarpaulin is staffed by parents and other volunteers who cook and serve the food. The children and parents are joined by guests from nearby sheltered housing and by others who pay with cash or tokens which they have earned or been given. All of the children have been involved in growing at least one part of the summer dinner today. Herbs, tomatoes, potatoes, lettuce, raspberries and strawberries all come from the school's or the centre's gardens. The children are encouraged to bring in contributions to the menu from home – a bag of carrots or onions, or some scones, or jam.

A sign reads:

EASTERHOUSE SUMMER KITCHEN
Children under 11 and guests free
Payment by cash or voucher otherwise
MENU Thursday 13 July
Summer vegetable soup
New potatoes
Tomato chutney, cheese, salad
Green beans and with garlic
Rhubarb and oat crumble

As the children, having eaten, go off to play, or to read, or water the plants, the adult helpers sit down to eat their dinner and tell their stories. Lauren is as thin as a greyhound, narrow, nervy. She rarely stops moving, always has something to do, something to set to rights, to see to.

'In 2012, I was 26, with three children under 8 years old. Nae money, nae life. I wisnae the only one. There we all were, in our wee flats or our wee houses. Nowhere for us to go that didn't cost money. We had nothing. We couldnae even afford the community centre coffee, that's how poor we were. Well, of course now there isnae any coffee anyway, and we still can't afford it. But back then, you could sit in your house all by yourself for days at a time, saving money with the lights off and the heat off and the telly off so that the power card lasted for the kids after school. I used to march the weans past the shops when we walked back from the school going, "Don't even look. I've nae money, you'll just torture yourselves. There's beans and breid till payday, and that's that." There were plenty of us in the same boat. So when the centre came up with the idea of an allotment – we were, like, "What? Grow things in the mud and eat it? Aye, that will be right. The weans'll get poisoned and we'll have the child protection onto us." But then we went, "Well, it's do it or starve." We had no bloody clue at first, but there was some of the older yins minded how, and we had the internet, and the library, and soon enough we were pulling some food out of the ground. Magic. You felt you'd got one over on the world. Food was free if you put in the work. We all started at it. The adults, the children, old yins, young yins. We did compost-ing, and we put in some cold frames, and we learned. Then there were more and more people wanting to join in, so we began to think a bit bigger. There was the land going to waste all round the centre and the school – all round the area, really. And now look . . . there's allotments, huts, picnic tables, fruit trees and our kitchen. That kitchen, I am out here far more than I am at home. With all my pals, my family, and my kitchen . . .'

Sitting with Lauren and the other adults is Rosemary, who feels more than a little satisfaction and quite a lot of surprise too, as she sits here on this summer's day, eating and chatting, and planning what needs doing next.

'I've been working the centre here for over 30 years. And lived here for longer. That was one of the big differences between us and people who used to work here. They came in at nine and went home at five again. What was supposed to regenerate Easterhouse was just going out of the area in salaries. There were the community regeneration team, the housing workers, the health workers, the social workers and the teachers. Easterhouse paid a lot of mortgages off all right. But our centre was started with the belief that the best people to work in the community are from the community. The ones that would come in and go home again, they were not here at the weekend or in the evenings. People were just left to get on with it. As Lauren will tell you, there were children going home to cold houses with no food. There were young folk hanging around, fighting one another, doing drugs, drinking. It's a lot better now, a lot better. Even children whose homes are not what they should be, they have safe places to come to, they have good food to eat. This is a much healthier place today than it was, in all ways. We have gone and regenerated ourselves, so we have. But listen to me blethering on! All this talk does not grow any tatties. On you go, and see what else you can see.'

*

Moving on towards the centre, through Shettleston, Bridgton, Parkhead, Tollcross, you will find the same story. Every bit of ground used. Areas that were wasteland, full of plastic bags, dog shit, human shit even, Durexes, broken bottles, cans, fag ends. The streets are clean: no glass, no gum, no rubbish. The gardens and balconies and windowsills are full of greenery. All is different and fresh and renewed.

You want to know more about how it started? And the problems we might have had? Let's go to the People's Palace on Glasgow Green. Where else would the heart of Green Glasgow be? On the north bank of the Clyde, near the centre, Glasgow Green is common land, owned by the people for grazing, washing and drying clothes, growing, playing; the site of speeches, concerts and fairs. Now, the Green has been returned fully to the people, for growing, and grazing. A salmon fishing hamlet in the sixth century on the Molendinar burn, which ran into the Clyde here, is believed to have been the first settlement in what was to become the City of Glasgow. The Clyde once again hosts salmon and other fish, and some fishing is allowed from the banks on the Green. The People's Palace, museum and café, is now the headquarters for SAS: Sow and Survive. The conservatory here is no longer a café but is used for growing and cultivating hardier versions of Mediterranean fruits and vegetables – tomatoes, hot chilli and bell peppers, melons, aubergines and avocados. Above the front door of the palace is a banner saying 'Who Digs Wins! Sow and Survive!'

Eleanor Murray is working in the main office, a well-organised space with charts marking out green sites and potential developments. There are screens, webcams and online communication all across the city and links with green cities all round the world. Eleanor clears a space at the table and offers us cold mint tea to drink and fruit flapjacks.

'You want to know about the start of it, and the problems? Well, you have the right woman here. Before this all kicked off, I was involved in environmental campaigns. A tree hugger, as they used to say! They said we wanted to go back to the past, that we were against progress, but it turned out they were living in the past, and we were progress.

We have had a few bad years with the weather, and that is not going to get any easier, but we seem to always come up with solutions. Even the big environmental problems, like flooding and storms, can be turned into an advantage of sorts with the right technology. You'll have heard that the university here has just patented a new material. It lets light in so it acts like a glasshouse, but it's strong as metal, and flexible like plastic so it doesn't break. But the exciting thing is it can trap rain power and turn it into heat or other energy. It's going to be a major export for the city, so that should boost trade a good bit. So, I'm optimistic about the technical side. It's the problems with people that could drive you mad. I think I have been involved in every single battle we've had. And that counts all the internal ones.

I always tell two stories that show what we were up against at the start. One is about the campaign against the M74 extension, which we lost. But the developers had agreed to consult the community about the green space they promised. I suggested that instead of the beech trees they proposed we should plant apple trees. This guy – council I think, but he might have been a developer – stared at me like I was crazy, and then he went, 'Are you stupid?' I said, 'No, I don't think so. Why?' So, then he goes 'Why? Why do you think? Because they would just eat them!'

Imagine! Free food! Children just eating it! Civilisation under threat. You might be thinking he was worried about whether the apples would be safe. But no. It was a good fifty metres back from the motorway. And anyway their case was that the motorway was perfectly safe.

No, he was just outraged at the thought that 'they' were going to get free food! How mad is that? He just could not get his head round it.

But now we have the fruit trees, and we have allotments, and a green gym, and rope slides and stuff. The motorway is only open once a week for the permitted driving day. The rest of the time, it's cycles and skateboards. And the children can eat as many apples as they can grow there.

The second story is just as ridiculous. There was Glasgow, with the worst health record and the worst diet in Europe. There was violence, drugs and too much drink. And that was just the councillors.

So, when the whole grow-your-own thing took off you would have thought they would have been delighted at the demand for ground. Not a bit of it. First of all, there was a rule they dreamt up that you had to be employed to get a council allotment. Otherwise, they said, the unemployed would be at work on them, growing free food, with no incentive to find work. They thought it was better for all the young people to be in training centres writing CVs, or in training to stack supermarket shelves.

That's just two stories, but there have been others. One was they wanted to shut us all down because of some food poisoning cases. I'm not saying you take that lightly; we don't. But the solution is putting the information out there about the right ways and the wrong ways to do things, not shutting everything down.

You would have thought that growing your own food was as dangerous as handling nuclear waste. From them having only one guy dealing with allotments, there was suddenly an army of people going round closing everything down, threatening to prosecute folk for growing food for themselves and their neighbours.

Look at the alternatives – cancer, heart disease, low birth weight, malnutrition. Growing our own is very low-risk by comparison. The biggest challenge we have now is in growing enough, whatever the elements throw at us.

Now, I have to get on with things here. You take yourselves up to George Square and find out what's going on up there. You can see the market, and you can go into the City Chambers to find out what the talk of the day is.'

Let's leave Eleanor to her potting and planning and go to George Square, the heart of the city, where all sorts gather to sell, to gossip, to complain and quarrel, to argue and settle. In the Square, and down Queen Street, and into Exchange Square, there are stalls selling not just food and produce, and gardening equipment, but also kitchenware, clothes, gadgets – everything under the sun. Currency is a mixture of 'real' money and local 'Greenpay' vouchers, which can be obtained in exchange for work, goods or services. Fine cotton towels and bed linen, dinner sets, stainless steel pots and pans, crystal glasses, canteens of cutlery, can all be bought or exchanged alongside spades, twine, wellies, plant food, seeds, plants, wheel barrows. And so, also, in quieter corners, can marijuana and home-made alcohol.

The biggest trade is in plants and gardening equipment – bug-resistant plants, trays of seedlings for those who have not the skill or the patience to grow from seed, safe fungicides, glass and plastic cold frames. And food, flour and oats are brought in by train from the surrounding countryside, or further afield. Bread, rolls, cakes, wine, beer and juice are all on sale as you graze the market. When you have had your fill here, the City Chambers provides a rest.

The City Chambers sits on the east side of the square, its stony great face boasting of the city's riches from its days of empire. Blood red marble inside; white cold face to the outside. For over 130 years it has watched the goings on in the Square and held to itself the whispering and manoeuvring and betrayals inside. Now it, too, has been renewed. People flow in and out of and around the building, letting the good air in and the bad air out. Many decisions are now made locally, closer to the ground. Now, the old council chamber, unused for much of the time before, is an open space for lectures, debates and speeches.

Liz Burns is in her regular place in the hall. She's well known here. Liz used to be one of the city councillors. She got a bit frustrated with committee meetings, and she and some like-minded citizens set up the Allotment Bandits: a retired chief constable, an ex-gang leader and one of the best lawyers in the city. These Robin Hoods claimed land all over the town, using every law and every lever they could, and handed it over to local folk. They were charged, threatened with violence, deplored in the Parliament and the press. But the Bandits defeated everyone and everything that stood in their way. Now, Liz is a fair age and she dwells on the past quite a bit. She comes back to the Chambers most days and, like the old politician she is, will give anyone who is around the sharp edge of her tongue.

'You've come to hear how it all came about? And how to do it for yourselves? Well, the first thing I will tell you folk is this – we didnae do it with a bloody strategy! Do you know how many strategies we had in Glasgow in 2012? No, and neither do I. We never counted them. But too many. Too many to read, never mind to implement. I kid you not. We had strategies for play, regeneration, community safety, parenting, anti-social behaviour, harm reduction, leisure, suicide, dementia, fuel poverty, care in the community, homelessness . . . That enough for you? Well, it wisnae for us. Oh no. We had strategies for excellence in everything, for reducing crime, mental health, physical activity, oral health, breastfeeding . . . We had an equality strategy. Everyone had to have an equality strategy. Equality was the law so they said, but not for food or money or housing or education. So everything got more and more unequal.

There were people writing strategies in government, in every department of the council, in the health board, the housing agency, every wee charity or trust that tried to draw breath. There were strategies for evaluating the impact of strategies. There were hundreds of meetings, minutes and records, reports, committees and commissions.

None of them were any damn bit of use at all. Except for

keeping some folk in a job, including me. Better than no job, which is what a lot of people in this city had. No job, no hope and really bad food.

Of course, in the recession, governments could only afford strategies. In the fat years, they would rub regeneration funds into sore places like Glasgow. Hundreds of millions of pounds. Chicken feed to the banks maybe, but still a lot of money over the years. But even then there was damn all regeneration. Somehow the funds never worked. The poor stayed poor.

Some folk made a good living out of it all, in the fat years, and in the thin years too. Regenerated their own bank accounts. It kept the mortgages paid for some, the airports and package holidays, the multiplexes, the restaurants all going. In 2012 we had strategies and we had services; we were turned into a country of people that just used services. Public services, or private services, we were all service users, or customers, or clients, but we produced nothing.

There we were in 2012, rich in strategies, but still, or because of them, the sick man of Europe. Still with the worst health, the highest mortality rates. Glasgow was the butt of jokes, the cause of shame and despair. Our babies were born too early and too small, with the shortest lives and the worst rates of cancer and heart disease in Europe to look forward to. There were generations of unemployment and illness in some families in some areas.

And there was the food. The food we ate was terrible. White bread, processed meat, deep-fried everything, drinks, sweeties and cakes made of sugar and chemicals. The alcohol was cheap, cider was cheaper than juice, and bottled water dearer than fizzy drink.

So how are we now the most sustainable city in the world? We woke up and smelled the coffee as we used to say in 2012, when there was a lot of coffee to smell.

The best I can tell you is that the roots of the change were there, even then in 2012 when things were at their worst. In fact, the roots were in the very dirt of how bad things could be. The roots *were* how bad things can be. We just woke up. And that is how the Allotment Bandits and a whole lot of other good groups got going. Come back another day and I'll tell you about that.'

Across the Clyde in Woodville Street, near Ibrox, below the high flats and in the wasteground beyond that, a small co-operative farm has been created, run by local people, mostly young men and women. Ten years ago this ground was 'No Washing' and 'No Ball Games', green but useless grass, an opportunity gone to waste. Now it is laid out in small fields, each with a crop, some with plastic poly tunnels, and all round the edges, herbs, flowers, cherry and apple trees, raspberry canes and blackcurrant bushes. There is a fenced-in sports pitch to one side, and to the other a picnic area with tables and barbecue pits. There is a market stall, selling whatever produce is available on the day.

Paul and his friends sit on old plastic picnic chairs at the door of a large shed. A sign 'Woodville City Farm' hangs on the door with a laminated 'Green Glasgow – Safe Organic Produce' certificate beneath it. They are all young – Paul, Magda, Julius, Linda, Bobby and Bruno – the Woodville City Farm Crew; hands dirty and rough, boots muddy. Paul is always the first to talk.

'I was nineteen in 2012. My life was nothing but drink, drugs, fighting, stealing, the courts and prison. That kept the bizzies and the briefs and the screws all busy too, of course. Useful employment for us all, eh? I was sick of it all but couldnae see a way out of it. I had a baby with my girlfriend, Linda, wee Frankie. He's eleven now, fantastic boy, my best pal in life. Great wee footballer too. But back then he was just a baby. I kept looking at him, thinking, Will his life be like my life? My dad died the same year he was born. Cause of death: Glasgow. Would I go that route too? So I was thinking, thinking about what life was in front of me. When the guerrilla gardeners as they called themselves started digging up and planting up the bit of wasteground up next to the flats, I thought it was crazy, a bit of a laugh, but I used to take the wean up in the pram and just stand there watching. It minded me of when my dad used to take me up to his dad's allotment in Springburn. He had a wee hut, and there was always tea and a bit of grub on the go. I have a photo of the three of us. My dad looking young – handsome like me, of course – nice clothes, happy. Like he was hopeful about things. But then my granda died, and that was it for the allotment. But I minded picking and eating blackcurrants and raspberries, and once my granddad washing a carrot for me to eat raw. But I wouldnae touch it because it came out of the ground. Crazy, eh, we didnae realise that that was where food came from, out of the ground, and that you could get it for free. We thought that anything that came out of the ground couldnae be any good.

So anyway, what with one thing and another, in the good weather, that spring, in 2012, somehow I ended up digging away too with the bandits and the guerrillas and that. So did other folk. Some of my pals started coming, and some of the asylum folk that had been put in the flats. That's how I met Julius. My other best pal in life now. Whatever it was, if they could grow it, they would grow it, and they would know how to cook it too. Linda and me, we hadnae a clue about cooking really. If it didnae come out of a packet with instructions then it couldnae be cooked. But we learned. So it just went on from there. Food got dearer in the shops, and scarcer too, but we had food for free.

When we had trouble from the local kids, some thieving, stone throwing, we just opened the door to them. We told them. Here you are, it's yours. You can fuck about and make a nuisance of yourselves or you can get intae it. We had a sign – 'Food for free. If you help grow it you can eat it'. Now some of thay wee tearaways are running their own fields, or wee businesses, and they keep telling us they're better at it than us. They fucking are too, but we're not telling them that. Anyway, Magda's the brains of our outfit. Well, that's what she says, and she keeps the books so we don't argue with Magda . . . Gonnae tell them your story, Magda?'

Magda, in headscarf and boots, sits with a small laptop computer on the table in front of her.

'Well, thank you, Paul, so complimentary. But of course I am not the only brain here, there is my husband too! I trained as an accountant in Poland. Don't ask me why I came to Glasgow. At first it was a shock to me, how people lived here. The dirty streets, the bad housing, the very small wee people. Bad teeth. The bad food. I met Julius here – he is from Uganda and not from Glasgow so he is very handsome and tall. Yes, Paul, only joking, some Glasgow boys are tall and handsome too. Now we have two children, both wee Glaswegians. They get a hard time sometimes – there are still some bad attitudes about different skin colours. From Poles most of all sometimes. But less now. And finally I got to be an accountant and not a cleaner! I do the books for three co-operatives. Two co-operative farms and our jam and pickle co-operative. Members bring their produce and it gets weighed, and then they get a share according to how much they bring and how many hours they put in. Julius and Paul take care of this co-operative here. And we are helping other people to set up co-operatives in more places, outside Glasgow now. In the summer we do work hard, the children go to school and then come to play here near us. They do their homework here. We cook out on the barbecue pit. Potatoes, beans, onions, scones, chapattis, chutney. Like Paul said, we just tell everyone, there's no point in stealing it. It's everyone's earth, everyone's food. If you help to grow it, you can eat it.'

But not much time now till the sun goes down. So, *whoosh*, back across town from the north-east to the south-west, to Pollock, to the Glasgow Girls allotments. Here are the girls, some in hijabs, some without, working away together in a large allotment, created from wasteground near Darnley Street.

Nusra is in jeans and hijab, her feet bare and muddy. She is planting out rows of parsley, coriander, sage and curry in raised planters that sit on a bed of gravel chips for drainage.

'I am a Glasgow girl. Me and my friends and some other girls have our own allotments here. It's not just for Muslim girls, it's for Glasgow girls. Me and Evie here are the main organisers, the bossy ones! No boys allowed, and no men allowed. No mums allowed either except by special invitation. Well, I do bring my wee brother sometimes. I like just coming here at the weekends and the evenings, and we just talk, and do things together. It feels really good to be able to take food home. And we even have a stall sometimes at the market selling curry and other stuff from our own vegetables, and we make some money. The worst times we had were the two summers when it rained and rained, and we could not get out much. The crop was poor then. And one time when all the wee seedlings got eaten by bugs. But we are much smarter than the bugs now. And we have even got round the rain and the droughts too. We build up the beds and use lots of gravel below so that the water drains off quicker, then we trap the rain so that we have water when it is dry.

I am going to be an energy engineer and build rain farms and wind farms. But I will still come back here. To the girls' allotment.'

Evie, her long dark hair tied up out of the way, is tying up the peas and picking ripe pods.

'I am a Glasgow girl too. I used to be a vegan who did not like vegetables, and now I am a vegetarian who likes chicken. There are still some vegetables I don't like. But I like growing them anyway. At first you don't think it will work, but it does, like magic. You put seeds in the ground, and then up come the plants. And it's nice to come here and be just with girls. Boys can be very silly and they don't work hard enough. And as well as growing stuff, I like to draw the plants, and the other girls working, and the slugs and insects. Before we kill them. The bugs, not the other girls. We had an exhibition at school last year of our drawings, photographs and the history of the Glasgow Girls Allotment, and it won first prize in the Glasgow Schools Green Art competition. Next year it is art school for me, but I will still come here. Unless us older ones get thrown out by the younger girls. They are really scary, that lot!'

Leaving the girls, going back across the river and out west from Charing Cross out through Kelvinside, past the Botanic Gardens on both sides of the Great Western Road, in the grounds of the University, in Kelvingrove Park, and outside the Museum and Art Gallery, we find the same. Food is being produced from well-tended ground, in gardens and parks, on unused land, in oil drums and raised beds, in school playgrounds, in hospital grounds. University students eke out a living growing their own, and working in the cafés and restaurants.

Further out west, in Knightswood, the park is now a patchwork of allotments, but the little burn is still a tadpole heaven for children. Every garden has a vegetable patch. The park café is back, and business is booming. And westwards, in Drumchapel, they specialise in berries. You can spend a morning picking your own from the bushes and canes, or you can go to the market and buy raspberries, strawberries, blackcurrants and blackberries by the punnet.

Fish in the river. Food in the ground. On both sides of the river and from north to south, east to west, Glasgow is flourishing, a dear green place again.

How did it start? As this story ends. Press *enter*.

Salanntùr

Caroline von Schmalensee

As you come over the hill and head down towards Salanntùr Research Station, the tower makes itself felt. Just south of Cape Wrath, at 300 metres high the building that has given this bay its current name – Salt Tower – stands, white and proud, off the beach. The fine mist of seawater it sprays into the air has changed the environment here profoundly in the last thirty years. Once covered in succulents and grasses, the beach is now a salt desert. White crystals sparkle in the sun and crunch under foot.

But Salanntùr is so much more than Britain's favourite producer of sea salt and an impressive tower. This tower is, after all, just a prototype. The data collected from it will be used to reduce global warming and justify the devastation of the local environment. Or so thinks Professor Arthur Mac, the man in charge of the Salanntùr project. A mile down the coast, he and his team are now working on a full-scale tower almost a kilometre high. It is the first in a flotilla of enormous towers that will float around the world's oceans to spray seawater into the air. The salt in the water makes the clouds more reflective so that sunlight bounces into space instead of warming the atmosphere.

The first full-size tower, Adam Tower, will initially float around Scotland. Once it is operating at full capacity, it and its crew will move down to the equator where it will be most effective. If the calculations are correct, Adam Tower and the nine towers scheduled to join it over the next few years will help stop global warming. They are Scotland's greatest gift to the world.

But it's a controversial gift. The project's supporters are excited about its world-changing impact while sceptics question the science and environmentalists are outraged at the impact to the area. To build Adam Tower, a large area of land has been cleared and stripped back to the rock. A new village, home to thousands of people, is growing in what was wilderness just a couple of years ago. It is difficult to estimate the effect on the local wildlife, but there's clear evidence of habitat destruction.

I have come to meet Professor Mac, see Adam Tower, and experience life at Salanntùr.

from Salanntùr – Global Hope? by Janet Wallace

Janet parked the car and got out. With her overnight bag on her shoulder, she went outside into the bright sunny day. Everything was covered in a fine white grit, from the walls of the garage to the bollards that led the way to the beach. She was surprised that the salt spray reached this far; she was several hundred metres from the research station. A tall man came towards her. She recognised Professor Arthur Mac from press clippings. He raised an arm in greeting and she walked towards him.

'Professor Mac?' Janet held her hand out and Arthur Mac grabbed it in both of his.

'Arthur, please. And you are Janet Wallace, the journalist?' They shook hands. 'Here, let me take your bag.'

Janet watched Arthur as he took her bag and started walking. He looked comfortable in his cord trousers and tweed jacket. His white hair was too long and whipped across his face as they turned into the wind and walked down to the research station. He carried his sixty-two years well but Janet did not feel the charisma she had expected. Arthur could have been any middle-aged man as he asked about her journey and commented on how lucky she'd been with the weather.

The sea was blue in the sunshine and the tower looked imposing where it rose up out of the water, wreathed in a shimmering mist. Janet recognised the shape, a narrow cone that tapered to a thin tall cylinder. At the top of the cylinder was a viewing gallery and a dome from which metal sprinklers protruded. They glinted in the sunlight and created a watery halo effect around the tower. Its beauty surprised her. Lights flashed from a mast at the very top of the dome, alerting low-flying aircraft to its height.

Janet could taste the salt in the air and feel it drying out her skin. It drained everything of its colour and made the bay painfully bright. Janet had been up since dawn, driving here through the countryside from Glasgow. Arthur was right; she had been lucky with the weather. Her six-hour drive had been glorious and she'd enjoyed seeing the green valleys and heather-purple hills. She'd seen deer, this morning, and she was sure she'd spotted a kestrel hovering over the motorway.

The science buildings looked rather old and tired. Professor Mac opened a faded red door for Janet and gestured her in. The small glass window in the door sparkled with salt crystals. Only the handle and the sign that read 'Salanntùr Research Station' were clear of the stuff.

They walked through the reception area and past several labs to get to his office.

'Have a seat and I'll get some tea organised. I've arranged for a driver to take you around later. Is that all right?'

Janet nodded and put her bag on the floor. The small room showed the tidal marks of lengthy use: layers of paint on the wall, islands of books and papers, a pinboard with mostly out-of-date notices. Janet could smell paper and stale tobacco smoke, and noticed where the carpet tiles had been glued down badly over old linoleum.

She was looking out of the salt-encrusted window when Arthur came back in, a tray with tea and biscuits in his hands.

'So, how do you want to do this?' Arthur said once he was comfortably arranged on his side of the desk.

'How about I ask you some questions and then you show me the sights?'

'Sounds good. I thought we'd go down to the beach so you can see the tower in all its glory, then to the saltworks, back here to the lab, then over to Adam Tower. We can have lunch in the canteen before I leave you at the building site.'

'OK. And where will I be staying tonight?'

'We have our own hotel. We're building lots of additional housing for the Adam Tower project. That's all happening over the hill, not here in the bay. You'll see that too.'

Janet unscrewed her pen and turned on her MP3 recorder. 'Great. Let's get started then. Tell me what brought you here.'

She knew the story well from her background research but it was good to start with something she and the interviewee were comfortable talking about while they got to know each other. She was saving the difficult questions for later.

The north of Scotland is not a natural place for a building project the size of Adam Tower. The landscape is craggy and wild, sparsely populated and has few resources other than water and wind. Yet it was these characteristics that brought Professor Mac up here.

In the late 1970s Arthur Mac, then a PhD student at Edinburgh University, was researching global warming. One of his projects involved using seawater to cool the environment. In 1980 he secured funding for a two-year research project. He came across this bay when looking for suitable sites to test sunlight reflection theories. After negotiations with the local council he got permission to use the land and had rented the site for a nominal fee ever since.

Salanntùr Research Centre, and the tower itself, runs on wind and waterpower. Before the Adam Tower project, there was very little infrastructure in this remote area. Home to about seventy-five people all year round, the site has been self-sustaining for over two decades. A farm a few miles away supplies dairy products, meat and vegetables to the scientists who live here.

Work on the prototype tower started in 1982. It was finished two years later and quickly became a tourist attraction. It is easy to understand why.

Only a little shorter than the Eiffel Tower, it is by far the tallest building in Scotland. The tower at Salanntùr doesn't have the filigree appearance of the Paris tower but looks more like an elegant helter-skelter. The 'thinking-cap', the popular name for the mass of sprinkler assemblages on the tower's dome, adds whimsy to an otherwise very simple structure. The only way up is via the stairs that run around its smooth white side.

'It's only a third of the height of the final tower,' Professor Mac explains, 'so it doesn't get the water vapour as high as we need it to go to be effective.'

The data collected by the team at Salanntùr is still valuable and gives them a good basis for projecting the impact of a full-scale tower.

'The tower brings two benefits: it has allowed us to work out solutions to a whole range of engineering problems, for example, how to avoid clogging and how to produce a fine spray with the minimum of energy.' Professor Mac smiles. 'And, of course, the profits from the saltworks have helped fund the research.'

The saltworks, originally a six-month research project in its own right, is now a profitable business. Salt cellars in the shape of the tower, with their clean modernist lines, have become very popular in recent years and are shipped all over the world.

On our walk around the works I grabbed a pinch of salt from the ground and put it in my mouth. I want to say that I could taste the grass and the sun, that the salt carried within it something that would always remind me of Salanntùr, but I can't. It just tasted of salt.

On a sunny day the salt-covered ground at Salanntùr is blindingly bright. But the salt here is concentrated, pure. It is difficult to imagine how salt molecules in water droplets too small to see can have much reflective power.

from Salanntùr – Global Hope? by Janet Wallace

*

Janet followed Arthur from the saltworks back to the science buildings, a plastic shopping bag with salt samples on her arm. 'The tower has changed things around here,' she said.

Arthur turned towards her and held his arms out. 'Indeed it has.'

Janet thought she could detect a note of smugness in his attitude. Arthur knew how few people could influence their world to the extent he had.

'You've built the tallest tower in Scotland, changed a beach into a desert, and built a research centre and village where there was nothing.'

Arthur nodded cheerfully. 'Those are only the changes we've made to the landscape. We've also filed 223 patents, published five books and, I can't remember the latest tally, some twenty scientific papers. In peer-reviewed publications, of course.'

'We?'

'The scientific community here. The tower might look like a massive sprinkler system, but it is rather more than that.'

They were back in the main building. Instead of going back to his office, Arthur took her through a door that led to a surprisingly large lab. One area was closed off by what looked like a large shower cubicle. The rest of the room was starkly white and well lit, with metal desks along the wall forming a central island. Five people worked in the room, all in white coats. Two men and a woman were tapping away on laptops, headphones in their ears. A woman with short blonde hair was bent over a microscope and opposite her was an Asian-looking man vigorously shaking something in a glass container. It was like walking into a stereotype of what science in action looked like.

'Anna Anderson,' Arthur indicated the blonde woman, 'has been with us for ten years now.'

'Ten years up here is a long time,' Janet said.

Anna smiled politely. 'It's not as long as some have spent here. I enjoy the work, and the company.' She nodded at her colleagues who were all paying attention now.

'Anna's work on clogging has been very important. She has three patents.'

'Four, actually.'

Arthur blushed. 'Forgive me . . . four patents.'

'Clogging?' Janet asked.

Anna opened a drawer and took out what looked like a metal drinking straw in shape and size. The top quarter, after the bend, if it had been a bendy straw, had hundreds of small perforations. 'The holes that the water is expressed through get clogged up. They fill with salt and impurities. It's difficult enough to go up and clean them on this tower, and almost impossible on a full-scale one . . .'

'The first few years we had to clean the sprinklers almost daily,' Arthur continued. 'Then we worked out a way to easily swap sprinkler assemblages out so we could clean them off the tower. Even so, it involved replacing almost fifty kilos of equipment every couple of days. Manually.'

Janet remembered the silver stairs that spiralled up the tower. She could not imagine climbing three hundred metres on slippery stairs to clean drinking straws. 'That can't have been a popular job.'

Everyone laughed.

'No, it wasn't. That's why we're so pleased with Anna's work.'

'So what did the rest of you do to be sent up here?' Janet asked.

A visiting student from Edinburgh piped up from behind her laptop screen. 'I specifically asked for this posting,' she said. 'There's lots to do here, and the work is really, really interesting.'

Everyone nodded. As researchers, their main motivation for being at Salanntùr was the work: interesting research and opportunities to publish. Janet had to remind herself that not everyone who lived here was a researcher. There was the staff at the saltworks and the various support functions – IT, administration and operational support.

'What about the non-scientific staff?'

'Some of them are from nearby villages. Before we came, there wasn't any work up here,' Arthur said. 'Some are partners of the research staff.'

'It's lovely up here, with the hills and the sea,' said Anna. 'We hike, fly kites, swim, and Jason has even got some surf in.' She indicated the man across from her, still intermittently shaking his glass container.

'The waves can get really big but the tower breaks them. It's a bummer. We have film evenings and spend a lot of time just hanging out,' he said.

'So what do you think of the new development?' This was the question she was interested in. To Janet, the new building site was a blight on the landscape and she assumed that its dramatic influx of new people would disrupt both scientific and everyday life.

'It's a change,' Arthur replied, 'but it's a change we've been working for.'

'Doesn't it interfere with life in the village?'

Jason shrugged. 'It's rare you get to see something this important coming to fruition. Of course it'll change things around here, but that was always the idea.'

'We're still breaking new ground,' Anna added. 'It's not like Adam Tower means there's no more research for us to do.'

'OK. Shall we go to the new village then?' Janet suggested to Arthur.

'Village!' Anna laughed. 'It's more like a town. It's got a pub!' She sounded more excited than disappointed.

As the Jeep took her over the hill towards the new development, Janet saw the old village and the desert below her. The desert was a white crescent in the bay, 500 metres wide at its deepest point. Janet could easily imagine a circle around the tower, described by the water it sprayed into the air. It wasn't a perfect circle because of the winds up here, but it was still easy to see this was not a natural desert.

The research centre sat at the edge of the crescent, a hundred metres or so closer to the beach than the old village. The village had grown around a few battered old stone buildings, the remains of a fishing village abandoned years before. Newer buildings of wood and brick were scattered across the hillside. Some were painted brightly, some left to weather until they were the colour of the hills. Gravel paths snaked between the houses, outlining plots. There were salt-blighted little gardens but no fences. The research station stood apart, a purely functional building, antennas, satellite dishes and what looked like a mobile mast attached to its flat roof.

As they reached the top of the hill the car made a sharp turn and soon they were travelling downhill again. Before long, the road, oddly wide and new in this landscape, levelled out. Anna had been right; this was a town, not a village.

There were building sites on both sides of the road, and as they continued they came to a square. The driver stopped the Jeep, and Arthur and Janet got out. The square was a clearing in a forest of four-storey tenements. Concentric stone circles of waist-high blocks created a space for walking and sitting. Flower beds were dug and waited to be planted.

The ground had been stripped of the local flora and houses planted instead. They were too new, to Janet's eyes; too tall; too out of proportion with the surrounding landscape.

'Welcome to the new Salanntùr!' Arthur said. 'Are you ready for lunch?'

Janet nodded and Arthur arranged for the driver to take her overnight bag to the hotel and pick them up after lunch. As they walked across the square, Arthur pointed out community buildings and other facilities.

'At the moment, we have over seven thousand workers,' Arthur said. 'They and their families need housing.'

'Everything looks out of place,' Janet protested.

'Out of place?'

'We're in the Scottish wilderness. There shouldn't be a town here. There hasn't been before. What does it do to the environment?'

Arthur shrugged. 'A lot, but not as much as you might think. We had to rehouse a few otters but the area will be returned to its original state as much as possible when we leave.'

'Leave?'

'The construction site will be gone in ten to fifteen years.'

'Really? The houses will be knocked down and the remains taken away?'

'The houses are modular. They'll be dismantled, not knocked down. There will still be a lot of rubble, of course, and we've excavated extensively to provide sound foundations for what we're building, but we're really trying to minimise the impact we have on this environment in the long term.'

'To you, this environment isn't very important, is it?'

'Of course it is, but unless we fix the global environment, the local environment doesn't stand a chance.'

Arthur opened a door for Janet and she walked into a large communal canteen.

Lunch reminded Janet of school dinners. It wasn't the quality of the food, but the protocol. Everyone queued politely, grabbed still wet orange plastic trays, and selected their meal from large stainless steal trays. The dinner ladies were friendly and polite. Janet chose pasta and salad. It looked nothing like the food she'd had as a child but somehow it smelled the same. She accepted a pot of jelly for nostalgia's sake.

Arthur found them seats with a view. They were sharing the table with a man in overalls who looked up briefly and nodded while forking a large helping of mince and tatties into his mouth.

'What brings you here?' Janet asked, deciding to forego introductions and launch straight into questions.

The man chewed and swallowed noisily. 'Lunch?' he said.

Janet laughed. 'Sorry, I meant here, to Salanntùr, not to this table.'

'I know. I was joking. Eh, work.'

'What work do you do?' Janet prompted while toying with some strands of over-cooked spaghetti.

'I'm a welder,' the man answered and stuffed his mouth again with a confused look at Arthur.

Janet tried a different tack. 'Where are you from?'

'Aberdeen. Used to work the rigs.'

'Do you have family there?'

'Aye, that's where we lived. Needed a change. So we came here.'

'To get away, do you mean?'

'No, to get work.' He sighed. 'Me and the wife were having a tough time. The girls are only wee and the shifts – two weeks on, two weeks off – didn't suit. There wasn't much work 'cept this.'

'You moved with your family?'

'Aye.' He downed his glass of Coke and wiped his plate clean with a piece of bread.

'How are you getting on now?'

For the first time, the man smiled and looked straight at her. 'Fine, we're getting on fine. It's hard for Shona away from her family, but she's no alone and she's made pals. Helps out in the nursery most days.' With that he stood up and made his excuses. Janet considered going after him to get his name but decided against it.

The work that the scientists and engineers at Salanntùr will be known for is not the prototype that stands there today but the big towers they are building.

'The effect Adam Tower will have is similar to when a volcano erupts and spews tons of fine particles into the air, except with salt water there are no poisonous compounds,' Professor Mac explains.

I ask him about the benefits of the towers over, for example, experiments with sulphur compounds distributed by aircraft that have been carried out in the United States and China.

'They're two sides of the same coin,' he smiles, 'but there are certain important differences. The first is political.

'Recent research has shown that geo-engineering, like social housing, is something most people see the value of but do not want in their own backyard, or in their own ecosystem. We are all for terraforming the Moon but are a lot more conservative about what we are willing to do with planet Earth.

'The sulphur experiments are carried out over land. They leave traces in the sky and there are a lot of people, particularly in the US, who are scared by what they see. YouTube is full of videos of so called 'chem trails', the long-lasting vapour trails released by the American research teams. There's a lot of fear surrounding them.'

'The sulphur spray can also change the appearance of the sky permanently. The addition of reflective particles high up filters out certain light frequencies. The outcome is that the sky will look less blue. The difference would probably be small but noticeable in rural areas where light and air pollution haven't already thinned out the colours that we can see. With the salt towers, that is not an issue.

'The towers will float in the middle of the sea, far from land. They do their work away from heavily populated areas. Their long-term impact will be the same but they will be less visible.'

The idea that the towers are less visible is difficult to accept. We're talking about towers almost a kilometre tall, floating on man-made islands. If they come within about one hundred kilometres of the coast, they will be visible on the horizon. The fine mist of seawater they pump into the air will look like low banks of cloud.

'They'll be easy to spot on Google Maps,' Professor Mac laughs, 'and boats will certainly see them. But the people most concerned about them – typically those in densely populated areas – are unlikely ever to see one.'

Whether the towers will be seen by many people or not, their effect benefits everyone. But one tower isn't enough; conservative calculations suggest that ten towers are needed for the project to have a significant impact. The most optimistic calculations suggest that a hundred towers would reverse the negative effects of global warming in a decade. Only the first ten towers will be built at Salanntùr.

'Ten will be enough to show a definite impact,' the professor says confidently, 'but we are running out of time. We need the cure to work fast: we need more towers.'

from *Salanntùr – Global Hope?* by Janet Wallace

Janet felt very small when she got out of the Jeep. They had arrived at the hangar where Adam Tower was being constructed. Five hundred metres long, half as wide and seventy-five metres tall, it was so enormous the houses they'd just seen would have fitted inside.

'You can't see it from this angle,' said Arthur, 'but only half the building is on the ground. The rest of it is over water; well, over a dry dock.'

She'd been close to buildings much taller than this one but never one with such a plain façade. It looked like an overblown shed. The blue door labelled 'Visitors' looked like a mouse's hole. She walked inside.

A tall woman in a hard-hat held out another hat to Janet. 'I'm afraid you have to wear this,' she said. 'This is a building site.' The woman introduced herself as Yvonne Owens, communications manager. 'I'm looking forward to giving you the tour – I've been practising.'

'Don't you get bored showing people around?'

'Actually, I don't get to do it very often. Considering what we do here,' Yvonne said, 'I'm surprised we don't have more visitors. It's a very special site.'

'Special how?'

'It's partly what we do – world-saving engineering, don't forget – but it's also *how* we do it.'

The hangar was bustling with activity. The huge room was divided into stations, some separated by walls, some just by walkways, where teams of people worked. It smelled of metal and petrochemicals, quite a pleasant industrial smell.

'So, tell me about it.'

Yvonne gave a brilliant smile and took a number of laminated flash cards from under one arm. 'OK. That's why I'm here,' she beamed and started her tour. They followed a blue line painted on the grey rubberised floor. It ran parallel to red and orange lines, and was crossed by lines in other colours every few metres.

'Normally,' Yvonne explained, 'a tower of this height would be built on land, bottom up. But we're not building a building, as it were, but a huge sprinkler.'

She flicked out a flash card that compared Adam Tower to the Burj Khalifa in Dubai, the only building of a similar height.

The floating tower looked very different from the rounded dramatically stepped skyscraper. Adam Tower stretched into the air, smooth and sleek like the wing of an aeroplane.

'It's aerodynamic, as you can see, and rotates to offer the least resistance to the wind. A tower this height needs a firm foundation to stand on. We've built what is essentially a huge raft that we'll raise it on. We're using technology developed for oilrigs to keep it steady in the water. Building a raft wide enough so something this tall won't tip over is impractical.' Another flash card showed the proportions of the raft versus the tower. 'And we're building top down.'

It took Janet a second to react to that statement. She snorted in surprise. 'What?'

'Well, the tower walls are relatively light and taper towards the top. Instead of starting at the base and trying to build each consecutive section higher and higher up, we start with the top section, then build the next section around it, like a collar.'

Yvonne pulled a brass spyglass out of her pocket. She stood it on her palm, lens down, and grabbed it firmly. With her other hand she took the eyepiece and pulled. The spyglass extended, section by section, until it was at its full length.

'Obviously, we're not pulling from the top but rather shunting the top section up and through the lower sections, but you get the idea. We'll add the pumps and pipes when the walls have been raised.'

'Wow, that sounds . . . complicated.'

'It is, but it's easier than trying to build 900 metres straight up on a raft. Come, I'll show you.'

They followed a pink line to the dry dock.

Janet got a faint feeling of vertigo when she looked down from the viewing gallery. The dry dock looked like a quarry partially covered by canvas. It was deep, wide and long, with rough stone walls. At the bottom was the raft. It was a ridiculous name for what looked like an underwater conference centre. On top of the raft, builders were milling around, building the third section of the tower. The first two sections had already been slotted together. The next day they would be hoisted up through the section that sat snug at their base, until they came to rest on it. The top of the tower went through the canvas that kept rain and wind from the dry dock, much like a flat tent-pole.

'There are ten sections in all,' Yvonne said. 'By section four, the top of the tower will be visible over the hill from Salanntùr Research Station.'

Janet was grateful to get away from the busy hangar and return to the small community. Despite its newness, it now struck her as safe and cosy rather than an impertinent imposition on the landscape. Perspective, she thought, changes everything.

Janet had hoped for something a little more distinctive than her bland hotel room, something that spoke to her about Salanntùr. Other than a small tub of salt scrub in the bathroom there was nothing. She took a long hot shower, enjoying the scrub, and got dressed again. She wanted the uncensored view of Salanntùr.

It was still light outside and the muted late summer sunshine made everything look rich and warm. Janet wandered down towards the square. It was a mild evening, the wind had died down and she hoped that people would be out and about.

As she walked past a coffee shop someone came out and locked the door. Janet stopped.

'Hi,' she said, with what she hoped was her most open and friendly expression.

'Hi,' said the young man as he put the keys in his pocket, 'did you want a coffee? I just closed.' He shifted from one foot to the other, thought for a second and put his hand back into his pocket. 'I can open for you if you like?'

'Thanks, but no, I'm not looking for caffeine. I'm looking for information.' She explained who she was and why she was in Salanntùr. 'Have you got time for a chat? I'll buy you a drink. And dinner.' Her expense account for this trip was limited but since the newspaper wasn't picking up the tab for the hotel, she figured it would stretch to whatever culinary experiences were available beyond the canteen.

Piotr, originally from the Ukraine, ran the new community's only coffee shop. He'd come to Scotland to study and had decided to stay. 'Scotland is a friendly place,' he said, 'especially here. Everyone's an incomer, you know. We're building something new together.'

It did not take them long to walk to the pub which was full of people. The whitewashed walls were hung with distillery prints and fringed with tall plastic plants. The building was so new it didn't yet smell of stale beer, just a lingering note of drying paint. A sturdy oak beam above the bar was covered in low-denomination bills from different countries. The pub had a buzz about it, a fizzing cheerfulness. There were no tables of people downing their pints in grim determination as in her local and no obvious signs of intoxication. The atmosphere was hospitable.

Piotr ordered at the bar and they joined four other people at a table. Janet was glad they were not on their own; this way she had more people to interview. Piotr introduced himself and Janet to the others. Because of his job, most people knew him. As they waited for Piotr's food to arrive, Janet asked what brought people to Salanntùr. As Piotr had suggested, they had come here primarily for the excitement of doing something new and being part of something that felt important.

'Compared to working on the rigs,' one man with a strong Norwegian accent said, 'this feels good. I'm doing something good. I use the same skills – do almost the same job – but we're changing the world forever.'

'So did the oil industry,' Janet pointed out.

'Yeah, but not in a good way,' the man said with a grimace. 'This is a chance to balance my karma.'

'Is that really how you think about it?'

'Yeah, and no. That's why I came here. It's a melting pot. Everyone's got a skill and everyone, a barista like Piotr, or an engineer like me, is doing something to save the planet.'

Piotr nodded. 'We're all in this together. It's like the army but without the rules. Focused.'

The Norwegian nodded. The woman next to him shook her head.

'Not for you?' Janet asked.

'Nah. I've never been in the army, and I agree that there is a strong, what do you call it, *esprit de corps*, one for all, sort of thing, here. But we're not soldiers, we're pioneers. What we're doing is revolutionary. And there are rules.' She laughed. 'Plenty rules! Without them the building site wouldn't function.'

'You make it sound like you're all cogs in a big machine.'

'I suppose we are. But the machine is grand, and we're very human, very individual cogs.'

Janet bought a round and excused herself. She introduced herself to some people at the bar and table hopped until the pub closed. Some people, like the welder she'd met earlier, were here purely for work.

'Life's not a charitable institution' said a fluids engineer, 'we can't just please ourselves and save the world. We need to pay rent and eat first.' But most of the people she spoke to agreed with Piotr and his friends. Life and work at Salanntùr had purpose and meaning.

As the engineers start work on fitting the third section of Adam Tower, I get ready to leave Salanntùr. When I arrived there twenty-four hours earlier I expected to find an industrial site, a ravaged landscape and a conflicted community. What I found did not meet my expectations.

It is true that the landscape around Salanntùr has changed profoundly since Professor Mac arrived. From a wild untouched beach estate it has turned into a large industrial site that stretches miles from the original bay. The placid green hills to the south of the bay are now covered in streets and multi-storey tenements instead of gorse and heather. The hangar where Adam Tower is being built, segment by segment, looks unfeasibly large against the backdrop of untamed wilderness.

Evidence of human habitation is everywhere: electricity lines, mobile phone masts, post boxes, handwritten signs for this week's pub quiz. People came here and made their mark. The changes that the last couple of years' dramatic growth have caused are perhaps irreversible, yet I am no longer sure that conservation is the only way forward. Radical change and progress has its place, even in the Scottish countryside.

People from all over Scotland, from all over the world, work together to build Adam Tower. They're creating a new world here, the kind of world many of us like to think we already live in: one where what you know and what you can contribute is more important than where you're from or who you know.

Salanntùr is a community shaped by science and built by scientists. It is natural that the people here seem rational and quietly confident. I'm not surprised to find a banner in the community hall that encourages everyone to 'Work as if you lived in the early years of a better nation'. The people of Salanntùr work hard and are proud of what they are achieving. Everyone works for a better world.

from *Salanntùr – Global Hope?* by Janet Wallace

At half past eight the next morning, Janet thanked the driver who had delivered her and her luggage back at Salanntùr Research Station. She met Arthur at the door.

'I hear you were in the pub last night,' he said with a friendly smile as they went inside.

'How did you know?'

'It was on the local news.'

Janet looked at him quizzically. 'You have a news channel?'

Arthur gave a deep and hearty laugh. 'No, the local news is what we call the community bulletin board. I always check it in the morning, to keep up with what's going on.'

'What did it say?'

'Oh, nothing bad.' Arthur took out a smartphone, tapped on it and handed it over to Janet. Piotr had written a short article about Janet's visit. It was a funny little piece of light-hearted gossip. It made her smile.

'These days there are lots of people in the news whom I don't know – I used to know everyone – but that just shows we're growing up. Did you get what you needed from your visit?'

Janet nodded. They agreed to talk in a week or so about some final questions and clarifications before the piece went to print.

'I hope you have a good opinion of us,' Arthur said.

'Would it matter if I didn't?' Janet asked, curious.

Arthur thought for a moment. 'No,' he said, 'it wouldn't. We have funding, we're on our way, so a bit of bad press wouldn't stop us.' He looked her in the eye and for the first time since they met Janet caught a glimpse of the charismatic leader who had made all this happen. 'But I'd hate you to misunderstand us. I want people to see the value of Salanntùr and what we're trying to achieve for the world, not just fret about the local impact.'

'Don't worry about that,' Janet gave him a reassuring smile. 'I've had a fascinating time.'

Arthur stuck his hand out to shake farewell. 'I'll send you an invitation to the Adam Tower launch. It will be quite spectacular watching one of the wonders of the modern world float out to sea.'

On her way back to the car Janet broke a piece of salt from a silvered branch of driftwood. It still just tasted of salt but this morning the taste was one of hope.

The Pleasure Palace

Kirsti Wishart

Since the Pleasure Palace opened a year ago scarcely a week has gone by without some scandal in the papers, whether it be the offering of designer drugs to teenagers, reported suicides by those who had reached their quota of visiting days or the rumoured orgies of the Pink Pavilion. Thousands, including myself, had signed a petition against the desecration of Rannoch Moor when its location had been announced. I'd argued in pubs about where the money was coming from, why it couldn't be spent on schools or hospitals and given a silent cheer at seeing footage of the 'Disnaeland' protest that had greeted its opening.

So, in the waiting room at Edinburgh airport reserved specifically for flights to the Palace it was hardly surprising I felt as comfortable as a designated driver in a room full of drunks. My fellow passengers had either paid a fortune to be there or were thrilled winners of their local Palace Visitor lottery. They'd been polite enough when I'd introduced myself but I'd felt a wariness when they chatted about the exhibits they were looking forward to most. I was sure this wasn't solely because I'd told them I was writing an article on my visit but because they picked up that I wasn't as giddy with excitement as they were. They were protective of the Palace and I think suspected me of being some kind of investigative journalist, determined to expose the terrible truth behind its creator, Guy Scott's propaganda.

But once crammed on to that tiny plane, sitting by the window next to Margaret Henderson, a retired primary school-teacher from Kirkcaldy, my cynicism waned. Perhaps it was the buffeting from Highland air currents but the reserve of the others lessened, their child-like enthusiasm, especially Margaret's, proving infectious. Her town had recently been selected for the monthly Palace's Gala Day and the pride shone out from her. One of the Pavilions, the Red, Red Rose, a massive exhibition space that usually featured major artworks by the likes of David Mach and George Wyllie, would be given over to celebrating Kirkcaldy at the end of the month.

'When I found out our town had been picked, well, I nearly *fainted*! There's going to be the usual King and Queen Parade but bigger, with the Bowling Clubs and the Ramblers taking part – they've made some *lovely* banners – and then the Guides and Brownies will be giving a concert, and we'll have people dressed up as figures from history and . . .'

'Look! There it is!' came the cry from the other side of the plane and without thinking we undid our seatbelts, trying to ignore the way the plane dipped, and the excited chatter died as the sight of it knocked the speech and breath out of us.

Seeing it from above, you gain a true sense of the scale of the place, the ludicrous Las Vegas-like ambition of it. I knew it had been inspired by the Scottish International Exhibitions of 1886 and 1888 that had taken up acres of parkland in Glasgow and Edinburgh, that Joseph Paxton of Crystal Palace fame was a hero of Guy Scott's but this . . . this was something else entirely.

An attraction the size of Dunfermline. That made the architecture of the Sunset Strip appear tame, as creatively adventurous as a Barratt bungalow.

It had been raining, the skies wild with shower-filled clouds but the sun broke through and those seven massive glass pavilions, the colours of the rainbow interlocking, surrounded by the bleak brown expanse of Rannoch Moor, flashed and shone, creating a shimmering halo effect. A dreamworld set in the wilderness, a glorious affront, a direct challenge to Nature.

The plane tipped, began its descent, and my palms began to sweat. With nerves or excitement I couldn't be sure but I had a fair idea the Palace was going to put up a decent fight against the cool scepticism, the ironic distance I'd planned to put up as resistance. Criticism could easily be overwhelmed by such glorious excess.

Once we got our feet on the ground, however, I felt a little more sure of myself. Down here the Palace seemed easier to cope with. That might have been due to the calming presence of the two Pleasure Attendants who ushered us aboard the small steam-train carrying us from the private airfield to the Palace. They were dressed in suits of light yellow, identifying them as experts in the contents of the Yellow Pavilion housing the Land of Cakes. A pleasant young man and woman, they had a composed assurance and unforced charm that set them apart from holiday reps or Butlins staff. In the days that followed, seeing how Attendants dealt with answering the same question asked for the umpteenth time that day, curing yet another panic attack brought on by excessive excitement or gently dissuading someone from getting *too* interactive with an exhibit, my admiration for them grew. Although now and again in conversation I would catch glimpses of a blank-eyed adoration of Guy Scott that left me with uneasy L. Ron Hubbard-like associations.

The closer we got to the Palace, the intersection between the Green and Yellow Pavilions, it became clear how referring to the Pavilions by colour alone scarcely did them justice. Scott had intended them to stand as a great memorial to the work of David Brewster, Scottish inventor of the kaleidoscope, each containing several thousand panes along a full spectrum of their colour. As clouds scudded, shades glinted, bringing to mind descriptions too fantastic for any B&Q colour chart: Buttercup Gold, Dandelion Sunshine, Absinthe Explosion, Emerald Ecstasy.

I'd been told there would be someone to meet me outside the Eden Garden of the Green Pavilion, and as I waved good-bye to Margaret and the other passengers practically running into the Land of Cakes, someone laid their hand gently on my shoulder. I turned to find a young Liz Taylor, her smile a little guarded, dressed in a dark plum trouser suit, white blouse, dark lipstick to match her outfit, black hair tied back in a ponytail, holding out her hand.

'Hello, Kirsti. I'm Gill, your Pleasure Giver. I'm the one who'll give you the tour, show you the sights. Stop you from getting lost,' and the tease in her voice as the Pavilions towered above us sounded a soft warning. Ridiculously, I found myself blushing. That phrase. Pleasure Giver.

No, not Elizabeth Taylor, but almost. It was the eyes that had got me, a quick flash of violet as the sun struck the side of the Pavilion, they had settled to a silvery grey. Her features were sharper than Liz's and there was a distinctly Scottish edginess, a sly humour below the surface. I knew as soon as I shook her hand I wanted Gill to be my friend and knew just as quickly that would be a bad idea. I needed to maintain a professional distance. I tried to focus, remind myself of underfunded hospitals, deprived council estates, food banks.

'Ah, hello Gill, this is . . . it's quite . . . something.' There was a pause as we both marvelled at my descriptive powers. 'Pleasure *Giver*?' I asked and Gill rolled her eyes, her smile almost conspiratorial. 'Is that . . . are you different from the Attendants then?'

'Yup, c'mon and I'll tell you. S'chilly out here.' She shivered, looking out towards the brown blank of the Moor before heading towards a glass door cut into the wall of green. 'The Attendants, they're there mainly to point people in the right direction, keep up general maintenance. Pleasure Givers . . .' She turned her head as she pushed the door open, catching my eye. 'We're trained to assess which areas of the Palace would grant the most pleasure to a visitor. When they arrive people can be disorientated. So much choice and only a fortnight a year to enjoy it in. We're here to make sure they make the most of their time.'

'So you tailor their happiness?' I asked, stepping over the threshold, and then Gill was speaking and I was trying to listen but it was difficult, what with having just found myself in a primordial forest.

Gill stopped, watched as I took off my glasses to wipe them free of steam. This gave me time to adjust to the shift from the brisk Scottish weather outside to this heat, this thick humidity. Once I had my vision back, could see properly the monstrous vine-covered trees and ferns surrounding us, the low-lying mist shrouding the undergrowth and glimpses of large animatronic flying things drifting above, she told me, 'Guy thought we should take you right back to the beginning. This is what Scotland used to look like, apparently. Before it all turned to coal. This way. Try not to wander off. Some of the exhibits out there have teeth.' She headed off down a mossy path too quickly for me to check if she was joking.

I caught up close enough to listen to her commentary above the chatter and call of extinct insects, living fossils. 'This is the more . . . exotic part of the Eden Garden. Mr Scott loved the greenhouses of the Botanic Gardens in Edinburgh and Glasgow when he was young, and this is his celebration of them. If we headed further west we'd come to the King's Forest section where there are deer and wolves running about – not real wolves but almost – then there are the allotments where prize-winning gardeners show off their vegetables and sheds and what have you, then the Tayside fruit-growers where you can pick your own strawberries and raspberries and blackberries. Dobbies has a section too where you can get a lovely cup of tea and a scone.'

I was glad of her chatter as it did a fairly good job of grounding me, having just stepped through a door in the Highlands and found myself cast back in time, straight into Jurassic Park. Occasionally I'd let Gill get out of earshot and stand on the path alone. But in that blue mist with the stillness of those trees surrounding me, the air would fill with a weird kind of tension and I'd get the sensation of something watching, hidden there. Something with teeth.

It must have been my silence that caused her to turn round and check. 'You all right?' she asked, looking at me closely. I marvelled at how she seemed to stay so cool in her suit while I knew my face matched the darker shades of glass used in the Red Pavilion. 'Fine, yes, just . . . y'know. A shock. This place. How accurate is it?'

Gill gave a kind of 'aw shucks' gesture. 'One thing you're going to find out about Mr Scott is that he never allows history to get in the way of a decent spectacle. Because if you were being strictly accurate you wouldn't see things like this . . .' She tugged at the branch of a bush covered with what I'd assumed were bright yellow and orange flowers except the flowers lifted and bobbed, flew around us in a mini-blizzard. 'Butterflies. Have you been to Butterfly World? It's outside Edinburgh. Actually, after this place, I wouldn't bother. They hate us, keep threatening to picket. Right, here we are.' I'm glad I was watching, hadn't turned my head to follow those butterflies, because otherwise I'd have missed her stepping into a giant redwood.

Which wasn't a giant redwood at all but rather a snug lift panelled in dark wood, red velvet and brass fittings, the sort you'd imagine Captain Nemo installing in one of his larger submarines. 'This will take you straight there, to Mr Scott,' Gill told me as she pressed a button in the shape of a golden arrow pointing up. I'd expected a slow ascent, a crunching of gears, but instead the lift moved with a stomach-lurching swiftness and I clutched at the guardrail while Gill stood calmly, arms folded. 'I'll leave you alone with him and collect you in an hour, OK? Oh, and he can be quite . . . intense . . . but he's like that with everyone. *Everyone.*' Although she must have been a good ten years younger than me, it was like a mum talking to her child before a visit to the headteacher.

Then the doors opened and there he was to greet us, the mad genius himself.

'Welcome, Kirsti! Come, come on, let's go to my office and have a chat.' He shook my hand with a surprisingly strong grip for a man so slender. He was dressed in his familiar light grey tweed suit, a homage to the artist Joseph Beuys whose pilgrimages to Rannoch Moor had first attracted Scott to this location. His round thick black-rimmed glasses gave him a look of perpetual cartoon-like surprise, emphasising the sharp angles and shadows of his face, and his black hair, cut short on one side with a fringe on the other, he pushed back perpetually like some absent-minded academic with a Bryan Ferry fixation.

He kept a grip on my hand while leading me out into a corridor that curved away on either side. The walls to the left were yellow, those to the right green, with dark wooden double doors in front of us that looked as if they might open on to a gentlemen's club.

'That's great, Gill, thanks. We'll see you in a bit. I was wondering if you could have a word with Angus in Cakes. He was muttering something about coeliacs, wondered if you had any tips.' Gill tipped him a salute and before heading off down the yellow-green corridor, managed to give me a quick wink as if to say, 'You'll be fine.' Which of course made me all the more nervous as Scott swung open the doors to his office and beckoned me inside.

I'd expected some clinically white affair, the room at the end of *2001*. I hadn't expected to walk into what felt like the inside of a huge kaleidoscope, transformed into the secret den of an obsessive collector of, well, stuff. Beneath a circular stained-glass roof displaying a colour spectrum was a large desk covered with books and magazines, papers and comics. Mexican Day of the Dead skulls, multi-coloured shampoo bottles, tin robots and Lego galleons filled shelves. As I settled into a leather chair while Scott sat behind the desk, a miniature train circled the room, making its way along tracks suspended from the ceiling. It tooted occasionally, releasing puffs of steam.

As my time was limited, I decided against niceties. 'So, Mr Scott, why the Moor? After all the intense opposition and the problems with logistics. I mean, the International Exhibitions you've spoken so fondly about, they were all set in the heart of the city, within a community, not a site of natural beauty, scientific interest.'

Scott tapped his fingers together, took on the look of a tutor instructing a reluctant undergraduate. 'Kirsti, I wanted the Pleasure Palace to be a place outside time, outside history, outside any given context. If I'd chosen one of the cities as a site, it would have been described according to those city's associations: a challenge to the conservative tradition of Edinburgh, a triumph of Glasgow's gallus swagger, a multi-coloured contrast to Aberdeen's granite façade. Here, surrounded by emptiness, the Palace is completely itself. It defines its own reality.'

And this was how he spoke, like a textbook on cultural theory given human form, his conversation ranging from the neuroscience of happiness to intelligent organic fabrics to what Walter Benjamin would have made of eBay. Much had been made of Scott's charm but I had the feeling of someone who had taught himself normal human interaction as a means of getting his own ends. I also knew that any opposition I voiced would be met with a quiet but implacable passion. He'd watched *Fitzcarraldo* over and over again as an impressionable teenager, and there was something of Herzog's insane ambition lighting the stare behind those glasses.

'But what about those who argue you've effectively created a Brigadoon, a fantasia of Scotland that distracts people away from actually dealing with the country's problems?'

Scott batted away the accusation. 'What people forget about that film, *Brigadoon*, is what a *wonderful* time people had there! The singing, the dancing ... The one bad thing about Brigadoon? The *only* thing? That it only appeared every hundred years. But that is also the thing that made it special. Made people want it. Look, Kirsti, I know this place makes you angry, upsets you. But that will change.'

It was like the director of a film suddenly turning the camera on the audience, and I stuttered a response. 'Angry? What? No, not at all, I'm only trying to find answers to the questions that many people have been asking. I'm a writer, I'm here to be ...'

'... objective, yes. Impartial. But I see it. Cracking your knuckles, the tension in your shoulders ... I have studied body language, Kirsti. Words lie but the truth, the emotional truth is told through the body. For centuries the Scots have kept the mind and the body separate. All that outdated nonsense about the split personality.' Scott made a noise almost Italian in its level of contempt. 'The Palace is about uniting the body and the mind, because only by doing so can true pleasure be found and most importantly sustained. Some people find that threatening, an absolutely radical exercise. You know, I have far more in common with those who protested against the Palace than many realise. We want the same things. A slice of heaven for everyone. Because if you give people a glimpse of that heaven they will work hard to build it elsewhere.' A significant nod in my direction and he continued, casting his eyes up, focusing on the splintered rainbow above his head. 'Giving people happiness can be a dangerous thing. It can also be joyous. A spiritual act.'

The train tooted nervously into the silence and I coughed. 'Yes, but, the money, where does it come from and the workers, where do they . . .' I was interrupted by a soft tapping. Scott stood up abruptly, took a few brisk strides to the door behind us, which I now saw was decorated by film posters for *Highlander*, *Local Hero* and Hitchcock's *The 39 Steps* and when Gill stepped in she gave me a look that told me she knew exactly how it felt to sit at the altar of Guy Scott for any length of time. Exhilarating and exhausting both.

'Ah well, here she is, Pancho to your Don Quixote.' I regretted not challenging that remark but suddenly wanted to be back in the company of somebody normal. Then at the doorway, shaking Scott's hand, an odd thing happened. A butterfly detached itself from me and flew up before settling on Scott's left shoulder. He watched it with such wonder that for the first time in our meeting, I felt genuine warmth towards him. Lifting his right hand he placed it in front of the creature which, as if it couldn't help itself, stalked on to his fingers. Scott lifted his hand carefully, examining its passenger, wings pulsing, as he spoke to me softly.

'It won't last forever. I'll see to that. Brigadoon, indeed . . . Have you ever been to the site of the Crystal Palace? All that glass and steelwork, all those displays, the gardens, the memories and now . . . nothing. Just dead grass and emptiness.' Shockingly, I saw tears brim in Guy Scott's eyes but he blinked and they were gone as he moved back, gaze still fixed on that butterfly, closing the doors behind him, still speaking but to me or himself or that insect I couldn't be sure. 'But when this place is gone, is given back to the Moor, the power of its memory will create miracles . . . Oh, there will be wonders when it's gone.'

'Quite something, isn't he?' Gill said, shaking her head as I turned in bemusement from the closed door. 'And now . . . relax. Fancy that scone now?'

'Good god, yes.' And as we both laughed and headed along the yellow-green corridor a very quiet voice in the back of my head reminded me, she's being paid, paid to do a job. She's not your friend.

In the lift down to the Yellow Pavilion I asked, 'Is it true you've been trained by the Red Cross?'

Gill raised an eyebrow, gave me that half-smile I'd already become familiar with, and a silent 'What do *you* think?' but I persevered. 'I've read Pleasure Attendants have been trained by the Red Cross in listening techniques. How to deal with people who've been severely traumatised following earthquakes, floods. Because Scots are so unused to intense pleasure that . . .' The lift doors sighed open and all rational thought vanished, swept aside by delicious sensation as the air turned so sweet it hurt your teeth to breathe it.

There was a scent of cakes and oatcakes, buns and bannocks, scones and shortbread so rich my stomach growled violently as if it would do me some damage if I didn't get out there and start eating. In a space the size of the SECC stood stall upon stall, stand upon stand, devoted to every kind of baked good Scotland had to offer from the best bakers in the country:

Fisher & Donaldson, Goodfellow & Steven, Ashers. I remembered a quote from a grudging piece I'd read that walking into the Land Of Cakes was like 'turning up at heaven and finding it sponsored by Greggs'.

I had to admire Scott's skilful blend of the monumental and the homely as some absurdly over-the-top display sat close to a stall offering practical advice on home baking. For every built-to-scale representation of the Forth Rail Bridge constructed out of Irn-Bru cans, split-level model Tunnocks Tea Cake factory that produced tiny tea-cakes or a Dundee panorama made out of fruitcake, there would be a Granny Masterclass offering instruction on how to make a clootie dumpling, tablet or meringues. I could happily have lost a tooth experiencing the nostalgia of the MacCowan's toffee section, Attendants stopped small children from licking the Scott Monument in treacle toffee or the vista of Edinburgh Castle made out of Edinburgh Rock. After we'd lined our stomachs with some Michelin-starred stovies and I'd tried not to think about how many sheep could fit whole inside the MacSween's Largest Haggis Ever Made, Gill took me through into the Orange Pavilion housing the Angel's Share and a walkable Whisky Map of Scotland.

'Every distillery?' I asked, eyes widening as Gill assured me, 'Every.' I felt a pang at my stay only lasting a week. We were met by Andrew, an expert in whisky psychology. 'You know Bach Flower Remedies? It's sort of like that. But with whisky.' Andrew was dressed in a shiny amber lab coat that seemed to darken and lighten in shade according to which distillery we entered, and as we strolled up the West Coast, past displays of copper stills resembling Anish Kapoor sculptures, he chatted away, asked us questions about favourite food, favourite colour, favourite cities, then angled us over to the top right of the map and the Ancnoc distillery.

'Here. This is it,' he told me, handing over the dram with reverence. 'Your newfound favourite.' As I took a sip of the sweetest smoothest whisky I'd ever tasted, I wanted, absurdly, to cry. It was probably the strangeness of the day but I suspected it had more to do with the level of attention shown by Andrew. Gill laid a hand on my shoulder. 'You see. This place gets to you, if you let it. Now, to the pub.'

Following an investigation of re-creations of some of the best pubs in Scotland, it took me a while to find my room in the Victorialand Hotel. Not so much because I was lost but because it was so pleasant walking those swooping corridors in sunset blues, pinks and purples, the alcohol drifting gently through my system. It wasn't until the day after that I realised the wall-paper had been moving, the walls decorated by a wafer-thin screen showing shifting patterns of colour and light to match the music of the Cocteau Twins playing constantly on the threshold of hearing.

Soft concealed lighting sensitive to my movements dimmed as I lay down on the bed. The walls were rich burgundy, the carpet claret, bedcovers dark scarlet, and I wondered how many Freudian-inclined interior decorators had been consulted to create this womb-like feel. But I was happy to have a respite from the sensory overload of the Palace.

I did groan though as I tucked myself between those wonder-ful sheets, looked up and saw the Northern Lights ripple across the deep navy ceiling. It seemed as if Scott's imagination was determined to invade the dreams of his guests. But it was with a smile that I slid into sleep murmuring, 'Ah yes, but is it heaven or Las Vegas?' as streamers of green and violet light faded above my head.

My hangover meant I probably wasn't quite as receptive to the joys of the Great Outdoors of the Blue Pavilion as I should have been. In spaces the size of film studios you could fish for salmon on a fake River Tay, walk to the summit of any Munro, snowboard down a Cairngorm slope through a combination of virtual reality technology and heavy-duty special effects. Perfect weather conditions could be summoned up at the touch of a button; a fresh snowfall feathering Ben Nevis, a crisp autumn sunrise dawning over the Old Man of Hoy, a light drizzle clearing miraculously to reveal the beauty of the Cuillins.

But it felt too ironic enjoying this uncanny valley when Rannoch Moor was, quite literally, on our doorstep. I pointed this out while standing on the shores of a sandy white Shetland beach, the temperature adjusted to a mild spring day and Gill tutted. 'But you've never been to a place like this before, have you,' she said, 'and seeing as how you can't drive, how would you get there?'

I was about to ask how much personal information she'd been given about me before my trip when she said, 'And how many people have the time or resources to venture to places like this?' She waved a hand towards a school of porpoises arching along the horizon. 'And then if they do go there might be storm clouds of midgies or it pours down or . . .'

'But that means the Palace sets reality up for a fall.' I picked up a stone, perfectly rounded, ideal for skimming, and wondered how many hours had gone into its selection, whether the set designer would be annoyed or pleased to see me pick it up, displace it. I threw it out to sea and it bounced once, twice, kept going, seven or eight times and I gave a cheer. And then realised I'd thrown a stone in a glass house and couldn't be sure if I'd displayed a propensity worthy of World Skimming Champion or if this was an example of the Palace tweaking reality, showing me what I wanted to see.

'D'you remember *Stars in their Eyes*?' Gill asked as she trailed a stick in the sand, turning curves on the damp surface.

'Course I do. "Tonight, Matthew, I'm going to be . . ."'

'That's it. Those performers, they were showing off the *essence* of David Bowie or Tina Turner or Freddie Mercury. Without all the baggage. They were more of a star than the star them-selves. And that's what this place is like. Scotland at its very best.'

'OK, but it's still fake, isn't it. I mean, it's not authentic.' Gill shook her head and was about to answer when a low tone began to sound, a sound not unlike an air-raid warning. Her face changed instantly, became older as she pulled a walkie-talkie from her jacket pocket. I overheard, 'Which sector? Nine? Evacuation started? OK, I'll be there in ten.' She dropped the stick and gave me a tense smile. 'Won't be long, sure you'll be able to entertain yourself. Some interesting rock pools over there.' And she was off, heading towards the source of that low threatening tone while I called after her, 'Wait, how long?' But she'd disappeared into the blue mist that shielded the entrances of the Blue Pavilion.

I should have followed her but I stayed put. Told myself I'd only get in the way as I walked over to where she had dropped that stick. It was bone white, the bark smoothed away after years of being pushed and pulled by the sea pulsing behind me.

Not that sea, the *real* sea, and I felt dizzy when I saw what she'd drawn. A labyrinth. A curling walk that took you back in on yourself, teased you with the possibility of escape but always led you back home. Kept you safe and contained without any hope of getting lost.

Gill assured me the next day that the accident had been nothing serious, a rock climber with concussion, but the spell had been broken. In the Purple Pavilion of the Play Ethic, I began to suffer an odd sense of vertigo. Too many realities stacked, teetering. Although a fan of console games I shied away from the virtual booths that allowed you to become a ninja or a pirate or a nine-foot alien overlord. Stepping into some fantasy world within a fantasy world without Gill by my side, I couldn't be sure I'd find my way back again.

'Right, well, there are the street scenes where you can play kids' games. They've got Kerbie or Hopscotch or Runnie-All-Over . . . no? Or there's sports. They've got these special suits and goggles where you can play at Centre Court or score the winning goal at the World Cup, a total fantasy for any Scotland fan, or there's . . .'

For one brief moment I wanted to be out of the Palace and on the Moor alone, but instead I said, 'Here, here's fine,' as we'd stopped at the entrance to Wonderland. A tribute to the old-fashioned seaside games arcade, the scent of fish and chips, candy-floss and cheap burgers wafted towards us while inside was the neon glare and blare of hundreds of different slot machines: one-armed bandits, roulette wheels, horse-racing, air hockey, penny falls and bingo.

I'd thought that the limits placed on gambling in the Palace would have lessened the appeal of such an exhibit. Visitors could buy the equivalent of £20 worth of tokens and any winnings could be translated into time. For every ten tokens won, an extra hour would be added on to everyone's yearly allowance of two weeks at the Palace. But the place was packed. Parents handed token after token to their children and watched as though hypnotised those paddles moving backwards and forwards, their faces tensing as tokens inched forward a millimetre. Something about the fixed stares of a row of OAPs at a bank of fruit machines, the mechanical way their hands dipped into the plastic pot by their side, caused me to turn angrily towards Gill.

'See that? Look. "Scott-land" at its most Scottish. It's like drink, it's like drugs, a short-term fix to take you out of it rather than tackling whatever problem you're facing. D'you honestly think there's anything here that will make this country better? Do you, Gill?'

She could have stormed off and I wouldn't have blamed her. Instead she looked at me thoughtfully and just when I realised I didn't even know her surname, she took my arm. 'Come on, time to take you to the Love Parade. Get you in the Pink.'

I'd shied away from the prospect of the Pink Pavilion, home of the Scots' Bawdy or 'Scots Wahey!' as it had been dubbed by the press. It was billed as an exploration of sensuality and the rumoured site of all those orgies. But once Gill had led me in there, it didn't take long for the nerves to fade away. The space had a delicious warmth to it, a Mediterranean feel, the light the colour of a sparkling rosé, giving everyone a healthy, happy look.

'It's only caused a scandal because the word "sauna" has

such negative connotations in this country. It's a Turkish bath at the back actually. And so what if folk were having orgies? Where's the harm? There'd be people on hand – don't snigger – to offer advice on contraception, techniques for maximum enjoyment.'

'Do you have to be so technical about it?' I asked, but I wasn't keen on arguing, not here. Large reproductions of J.D. Fergusson's joyous paintings hung on silk banners next to displays celebrating Scottish-inspired fashion – Jean Muir, Alexander MacQueen, Vivienne Westwood. Models, so stunningly beautiful they seemed a different species altogether, stalked around wearing exhibits, chatting with visitors about how they were made until a chime sounded every hour and they headed to the central catwalk where they gave a display of such camp theatricality the audience's applause was raucous.

A number of skilled tailors and seamstresses using the latest sewing technology could quickly construct a perfectly flattering outfit for visitors and to display it to their best advantage there were a number of ballrooms each with sprung dance-floors the size of the Barrowland's. Glasses of champagne encouraged the reluctant to join in a Strip-the-Willow, a tea dance, flamenco or samba lessons.

It seemed positively rude not to join a ceilidh and rediscover how complicated the Canadian Barn Dance was. Afterwards, pink-faced and happy, Gill took me to the perfume section where a scent perfect for your skin type could be blended. Mine smelled woody, musky and smoky, and I was sniffing my wrist, making sure the tiny bottle was safe in my jeans pocket, knowing the memories it would trigger of this place, when we reached the entrance of the Turkish baths.

A critic of Orientalism would have had a field day with the décor: the pink marble archway, white pillars, the decorated tiles, swathes of richly patterned fabrics draped from the walls, ottomans and chaises longues. I could see people wandering about in robes, silk dressing gowns, their faces flushed, expressions slightly dazed, blissed out.

'This is where all the orgies take place, supposedly,' Gill told me. 'Inside it's like a spa. Steam rooms, you can have a long soak, massages . . . and there are counsellors in there to help couples, offer advice. Doesn't matter what you are, gay, straight, trans, whatever, there'll be someone there to help you. Remember how the *Daily Mail* kicked off about the Gay Pride rainbow association? Well, they weren't so very wrong.' There was something wicked in Gill's smile then, a challenge. 'You were asking what good this place could do. Here we teach people how to give and receive pleasure. We're teaching them how to love properly. So, you going to give it a go?'

'You know, I would, honestly, but my glasses. They'd steam up, without them I'm as blind as . . .' But Gill had already given up on me, shaking her head, that half-smile teasing me.

'I don't know. Such a lot to learn,' she sighed. 'You got a partner, Kirsti?' And there was that feeling of being caught out again. 'Ah, sort of, but it's . . . it's complicated,' I managed, and Gill nodded in a way that told me she knew all about that. 'Well, bring them here the next time and it might be a bit less complicated. Now, come on, let's get your outfit sorted out for tomorrow, the final night.'

Trying it on in my hotel room, the black jumpsuit didn't look too impressive. But I'd been assured it was packed full of technology designed to maximise enjoyment of Joy Euphoric!, the Friday club night held in the central Red Pavilion, the Red, Red Rose at the heart of the complex. The fabric felt so light it was scarcely noticeable and it came to life fully once I was on the dancefloor the next evening, the art exhibits cleared away, hundreds of red glitterballs overhead, hundreds of people dancing.

Sensors and electrodes were woven into the fabric so you could feel the music. Lights and holographic projectors along the collar and seams reacted to sound and I became my very own lightshow as DJs Rustie and Hudson Mohawke played, a mad mash of video games sound effects and 80s theme tunes that sounded as if it had been mixed by an eight year old who'd eaten too many Wham! bars, the sort of music that could result in a new religion being born. I threw myself against those squelchy beats, the bass that hugged your lungs, that made you forget who you were, where you were, that tipped you into unalloyed sensation.

Perhaps it was because of my hesitation at the threshold of the Turkish baths, perhaps it was because I couldn't decide if I was ecstatic or miserable to be leaving the Palace the next day, but I didn't worry about taking the drugs that were offered, didn't care that they'd been specially tested in government-approved laboratories. Combined with the special effects of the suits they gave the illusion of people metamorphosing, a burst of light from a collar becoming a lion's mane, a flare of purple and green a peacock's tail. I would see Gill out there in the crowd, still wearing her plum-coloured suit, lost in her own dance, light bursting from her shoulders, transforming into a set of wings, a butterfly, a bird, an angel.

The crowd – all one, no sense of separation between us, pieces in a communal artwork. And I remember the laughter. The sound of people realising they were becoming more than they ever thought possible, everyone as spectacular and outlandish as the Pleasure Palace itself, true citizens of this mini-state.

I don't remember how I got back to my hotel room but I do remember lying on my bed, still in my suit, drowsing. A soft tapping at my door. I got up, head spinning, opened it and there was Gill. Beautiful Gill looking a little drunk, her lips and hair shining in the soft light as 'Treasure' played.

'So, Kirsti, your last night . . . Has your stay at the Palace been all you hoped it would be? Anything that you wished would happen that didn't?'

Those rumours about the Pleasure Givers. About just how far they would go to give the visitors what they wanted. What they needed.

'Emmm, well, there was that Coffee House you were going on about, y'know, where you could discuss Enlightenment stuff with David Hume over a latte and not catch smallpox or anything and . . .'

She leaned in quickly and kissed me long enough for me to taste the sugar from the pills she'd swallowed. Tiny detonations, fireworks of pleasure went off in the back of my head. Then she pulled back, watching me, enjoying my reaction.

And I hesitated. Told myself, this is a job, just a job to her but something in my chest ached, my throat tightened as I said, 'Gill . . . my partner. It's . . . well, it's . . .'

'Complicated.' She laughed, shook her head ruefully. 'Yeah, well, pleasure always is. Complicated. Right, well, be seeing you. You've one week left this year, remember. Better make the most of it next time. Because you've still got an awful lot to learn.' And she was off, swaying back down the corridor, trailing her hand along the walls, causing rosy golden streamers of light to follow her.

When I woke up I couldn't decide if what had happened with Gill had been a dream or not, sure only of the tingle on my lips. I sat on the side of the bed for a while, then got up, opened the door and walked those winding corridors until I found a fire exit. Slipping out towards the Moor, I was amazed at how easy it was to leave. Surely the Moor was a dangerous place, something we needed to be protected from? But I headed away from the Palace, testing myself, into the darkness. I kept walking, still feeling the euphoria of the club night, my ears still thrumming, face sore from smiling, relishing the breeze on my face, realising it had been days since I'd breathed fresh air, proper fresh air.

Then I stopped and knew I was lost. Surrounded by the cold and a terrible blankness I turned, once, twice, three times, panic rising until I saw a dim blue light in the distance. I couldn't be sure if it was the light from the Blue Pavilion or the sunrise but I headed in that direction, the Moor trying to trip me, to drag me down. I thought of Scott's words – 'When it's gone, there will be wonders,' – and I tried not to think. I concentrated instead on the ache in my lungs and tried not to doubt what I was running towards.

The authors

ANDREW CRUMEY

Andrew Crumey's novels include *Sputnik Caledonia*, *Mobius Dick* and *Mr Mee*. He has a PhD in theoretical physics and is former literary editor of *Scotland on Sunday*. He is currently senior lecturer in creative writing at Northumbria University, and is actively involved in mentoring emerging writers. He was winner of the 2006 Northern Rock Foundation Writer's Award; other prizes include the Saltire First Book Award and Scottish Arts Council Writers' Award. *Sputnik Caledonia* was shortlisted for the James Tait Black Award and Scottish Book of the Year; *Mobius Dick* was a finalist for the Commonwealth Writers' Prize; *Mr Mee* was longlisted for the IMPAC Award and Booker Prize.

MICHAEL GARDINER

Michael Gardiner is Professor of English and Comparative Literatures at the University of Warwick. As well as academic books on British literary and political history (particularly surrounding self-determination) and Euro-Japanese comparative literature, he has published one book of short stories with Polygon, *Escalator* (2006), and one biography, *The Edge of Empire: The Life of Thomas B. Glover* (Birlinn 2008/Japanese translation, Iwanami 2012). He has won a Scottish Arts

Council major award and many smaller grants, and had stories and books shortlisted for prizes.

GAVIN INGLIS

Gavin Inglis has been a handyman, teacher, busker, stage manager, PR executive and UNIX system administrator. His publications range from *Grunt and Groan: Fiction about Sex at Work* to *Crap Ghosts*, seventeen stories of substandard spooks. Gavin's spoken word has featured at the Latitude festival, burlesque events, the Edinburgh Book, Fringe and Science Festivals, punk gigs, Literary Death Match and a roller derby fundraiser. He is the producer of Underword, performs with the group Writers' Bloc, and his work appears on albums by Glasgow bands Spylab and Cinephile. His irreverent interactive fiction Eerie Estate Agent is available from Choice of Games for smart-phones, ebook readers and the Web. www.gavininglis.com

WILLIAM LETFORD

William Letford lives in Stirling and has worked as a roofer, on and off, since his teens. He used to hide his poems amongst the beams and joists of roofs where he worked. He has an M.Litt in Creative Writing from the University of Glasgow. He received a New Writer's Award from Scottish Book Trust and an Edwin Morgan Travel Bursary from the Arts Trust of Scotland. His first collection of poetry, *Bevel*, was published by Carcanet in 2012.

MAGGIE MELLON

Maggie Mellon was born in Glasgow, raised in Greenock and Dumfries, and now lives in Edinburgh. She is married with two sons in their twenties. Maggie had a long career in social work in London and Scotland, and is now on the board of NHS Health Scotland, also working independently with charities and local authorities on a range of projects. She is also a writer and talker, and works independently at various endeavours.

CAROLINE VON SCHMALENSEE

Caroline von Schmalensee was born in Stockholm, Sweden. She came to Edinburgh to study in the early 1990s and never looked back. After working as a technical writer and copywriter for many years, she returned to her first love: fiction. Caroline's short stories appear in *New Writing Scotland* and online, and she reads at spoken word events in and around Edinburgh. Caroline writes about writing at carolinevonschmalensee.com.

KIRSTI WISHART

Kirsti Wishart's short stories have appeared in *New Writing Scotland*, *The Eildon Tree*, *The One O'Clock Gun* anthology and on Laura Hird's website. In 2005 she was awarded a SAC New Writers' Bursary and in 2007 won a place on the Scottish Book Trust mentorship scheme. She is a member of the Edinburgh-based spoken word group Writers' Bloc and is currently working on her novel, *The Pocketbook Guide to Scottish Superheroes*. For more information please visit www.scottishsuperheroes.com.